Kings and Cowboys

J.A. Woods

CIMARRON RIDGE
WHERE WILD SHEEP ROAM

Cimarron Ridge Publishing

ISBN: 978-0-578-21174-9

Library of Congress Control Number: 2018913525

PRINTED IN THE UNITED STATES OF AMERICA

In loving memory of my big brother and my mom,
who taught me to persevere despite the cards we're dealt.

WILL: BETS AND BLUFFS

*Big Blind: Placing a high stakes
bet without seeing the cards first.*

— Dictionary of Poker Terms

I see him crank the steering wheel; the rear of the car fishtails to the left. From the back seat, I reach toward Vincent's shoulder, to tell him to stop showing off and get his shit together. My hand never connects. The back tires catch traction on the road, pushing us over the twenty-foot embankment. I watch my hand float up to the gray felt of the roof lining, then flail back in slow motion to my face. The car tips over the edge and the momentum pushes it onto its left side. I find my feet against the door, almost standing, looking downhill. I see nothing in the dark void. I lean over Rhonda to shelter her with my arms as we smash into the merciless bed of the ravine. Glass explodes beneath me and a shredding pain shoots through my shoulder.

The car swivels and launches into the shadows, tumbling in midair like a carnival ride. I catapult to the roof; then a crunching sounds inside my head. The car orbits again, slamming us into the opposite side of the cab. In a single action, the car door rips away and ejects both door and me into the waiting arms of the granite mountain. The girls' screams lace with the shriek of metal on metal. My brain doesn't register hitting the ground, but a terrifying scene unfolds in front of me. The car bounces wildly on all four tires, tossing the humans inside like limp ragdolls. Somehow, it stops upright. I clench my eyes to turn off the nightmarish movie. A strange medley of mournful wailing and mechanical hissing begins. Oily stench burns my nose. A bitter liquid spreads inside my mouth. Then, the world blackens into nothingness.

Where the hell am I? I'm freezing my ass off. I'm pinned under something, I can't move. I can't see anything. Am I blindfolded? What the hell? Suddenly, pinpricks of stars swirl above me. Underneath me, the frozen earthquake injects involuntary shivers into my back.

"I'm freezing out here. Vincent, where are you, man?"

"I'm here— I'm right beside you, buddy."

"I think my legs are broken," I grit the words through my teeth. "Where's Christine? Is she okay? Vincent?"

They should have let me lie still, but I was in such pain. I ask Vincent to put something under my head and that's what must have finished me off.

"Who—who is Christine?" A quivering, high-pitched voice sounds behind me.

"She's his girlfriend back in Cody. He—he must think you're her." Vincent chokes on his words as he grips my hand.

"The girls are going to try to get to the ranger's cabin and call for help. We rolled the car, man. You've got to take it easy. You're hurt, buddy. I'm going to help you, okay?" Vincent cradles my head, trickling some liquid onto my lips. It is rum. He's taken his flask out, hoping it will help the pain.

"Put my leg down. My knee is bent. Goddammit, it hurts! Vincent, put my leg down."

"I would, Will, but both your legs are already lying flat against the ground." The girls start crying and I think I hear Vincent sniveling beside me.

"Aaaaa-hhhhh-ggg." I follow my voice into the chasm, enveloped in black again.

WILL: CROSSROADS

You can't run away from trouble.
There ain't no place that far.

— Uncle Remus

"Ready!" yells the instructor.

Knees bent, I lean forward onto my toes, tucking my head into my outstretched arms.

"On your mark!"

I pull in a huge gulp of air and close my eyes.

"Go!"

I leap, feet losing contact with the concrete edge, then the cold shock as I dive underneath the water.

This is the moment I live for: propelled into liquid space, completely submerged, weightless, and silent except for the bubbles rushing past my ears. The outside world disappears and it is just me, my own thoughts, and the silk of the water on my skin. Gliding until my momentum slows, then: frog kick, sweep arms wide. I know how many strokes it takes to reach the pool's far side.

I sense the swish and swirl beside me, the other boys trying to keep up. On count seven, I open my eyes to the sting of chlorine and reckon how close I am to the wall. *Somersault, plant feet, shove off. Count to seven again.* Halfway back, lungs burning, I'm smiling to myself. The others torpedo to the surface for air, but not me. *I'm Aqua-Man!*

I'm eleven, maybe twelve years old at the most, hanging around with my big brother Dean and the older boys who are taking junior lifeguard lessons. The instructor challenges his students to the next drill. They are to dive to the bottom of the deep end and rescue a heavy rock wrapped in burlap. After the others are done, I ask if I can try it.

"Sure," says the teacher. "Go for it!"

I've watched some of them, and my brother had figured out how to push off from the bottom and swim like hell to the top. I could tell that he struggled to get it done, and a lot of the other boys couldn't hack it at all. I'm younger than them, and smaller, but I'm stout and strong. When the coach gives me the signal, I dive under, hook the rock, cradle it under my arm and push off the bottom, employing my dolphin kick to gain thrust. I pop to the surface and heave the rock onto the lip of the pool. Hands reach down and lift me out of the water. The mob cheers and above the din I can hear my brother's voice, louder than anyone. I squint, trying to spot him, but all I see is a form blocking the sun's glare.

♠ ♣ ♥ ♦

Foreign and indistinct voices invade my dream; I wrench my eyes open, trying to shade my eyes from the glare of what I still think is the sun. But my hand doesn't move, and instead of summer sun, sterile gray fluorescent bulbs spotlight me. Gowned forms and anonymous arms reach over me, at me, around me in a flood of motion. I close my eyes, feeling drowsy.

The doctor's voice intrudes. "You may feel a bump here."

I open my eyes as a mallet swings with a whack above me. My head quivers. Another whack and another quiver, this time on the left side of my head. Two surgical steel bolts have been hammered into either side of my skull just above my ears. The unnamed arms and hands fix curved, scissor-like tongs to the bolts, and two eight-pound steel bricks are hung from a rope, running over a pulley and wheel attached to something behind me I can't see. This, the mysterious masked nurse tells me, will stretch my neck vertebrae apart to relieve the compression on my spinal cord. The doctor peers over me into my face, saying that he needs to limit my head rotation to avoid further injury.

Mom, where are you? Help me! No one comes. Tears stream down my face. I can't raise my hand to wipe them off. *What's wrong with me? Why can't I move my hands? I can't feel my legs or my body. My mind is my only working organ. What the hell?*

Hours — maybe days — pass. I can't gage the passage of time, but flashes reel past in my mind's eye in a surreal dream state: freezing, lying on the ground, staring up at Vincent's face; ambulance lights strobe across pine trees; the sense of movement in utter blackness, then replaced by blinding white overhead; a hallway with voices echoing faintly along the corridor.

As I fight to climb up into full consciousness, my only thought is that I need to see my family. I sense someone beside me; she's sitting in a chair too low for me to look at her, but I know it's her.

"Mom, what's happening to me?" I ask the question, but I'm terrified to learn the answer. "Am I going to live?"

Startled by my voice, she stands and leans on the bed rails, then breaks down sobbing and holds her head in her hands.

"I don't know," she snuffles. "The doctors don't know either."

She draws in a breath, steadies herself.

She says, "They're doing everything they can, son."

The shockwave travels between us. Mom's face mirrors my hopelessness. Her eyes, diffused with tears, are dull. Her forehead wrinkles and the corners of her mouth draw downward. Her breathing has turned slow and feeble, interrupted by occasional spasms and deep sighs. A lump rises in my throat as the suffocating despair settles over us.

The nurse bustles into the hospital room, giving us

the distraction we need.

"I'm sorry, Mrs. Alves, you'll have to leave now. But visiting hours start again tomorrow at 8:00 a.m."

"Okay," says Mom, dabbing at her eyes. "But, please, just call me Beverly."

The nurse gently leads Mom out, steadying her and talking low to try to reassure her.

Later that evening, alone with my thoughts, despair settles over me again.

So. Here's the hand that I was dealt on May 22, 1966 at the ripe old age of seventeen.

My bluff was called by *Him. He* wanted to see what I'd do if I was tempted with some type of big payoff. *I should be dealt a whole new hand. Let me throw in every last card and draw new ones.*

I run the movie in my mind: Vincent and I don't skip out on the game; we don't take my car to Red Lodge. We don't pick up the girls and drive up the switchbacks to the campground. Instead, we stay in Cody that night, we cruise Main Street, maybe run out to the canyon to watch a couple of our friends drag race through the tunnel. We spend the night drinking some beer, teasing the girls, bragging to the other boys about how we're going to kill them in wrestling this year.

But we know that's not what happened, and now I'm left wondering how I came to be at this crossroads.

BEVERLY: TECTONIC SHIFT

Man never legislates, but destinies and accidents,
happening in all sorts of ways, legislate in all sorts of ways.

— Plato

Where is that boy of mine? It's two o'clock on Saturday morning! He should have been home by curfew at midnight. Just wait until Leon gets hold of him. He'll set him straight!

The phone rings and I jump, startled. My maternal antennas are on alert.

"Hello?" A call at this time is never good news.

"Mrs. Alves?" The woman's strained voice on the other end of the phone line calls me by my former married name. It's Landon now, but I don't try to explain.

"Yes, this is Beverly Alves."

"Ma'am. I'm Bernice Olson, the charge nurse in emergency at…"

Her words sucker-punch the breath out of me. The phone receiver slips from my grasp.

From the receiver on the floor, I hear her faint voice again.

"Mrs. Alves? Are you okay? Do I need to send an ambulance? Mrs. Alves?"

I struggle to reach the phone and put it to my ear.

"What — what's happened? It's my boy Will, isn't it?"

"Yes, ma'am. He's here in the emergency room at Deaconess Hospital in Billings. He's in critical…"

"Oh, my God! I *knew* something terrible was going to happen." Tears blind me; I get tangled in the covers trying to sit up, to find my slippers. *I need to go to him!*

I don't remember the hundred-mile drive to the emergency room, but I do recall the nurse who I'd talked to on the phone. She met me at the door to the ER lobby and asked me to sit down with her. The nurse explained that the injury Will "sustained" was "significant" and his "spinal cord was damaged." They weren't sure they could save him and asked me to prepare to see him for the last time.

I distinctly remember thinking: *If I don't follow her to that room, they won't be able to tell me that my son is dead.*

BEVERLY: WINDOWPANES

Life calls the tune, we dance.

— John Galsworthy

Our lives are reduced to those times when we stare out the window, mulling over what brought us to this point in our lives. I'm sitting here at my kitchen window in the yellow duplex in Cody, looking across the street at the post office. People walk in, then they walk out with handfuls of mail, which tells me that someone cares that they are alive. I decide at this moment that I will be diligent in writing letters, in the hope that I will get replies, that those I care about and write to will return the gesture. I vow to remember birthdays, to send a card, to acknowledge that soul's existence in this world.

One month ago, my son Will was in a terrible accident. He is in the hospital in Billings, a hundred miles away. I cannot be with him every day because I have to work. I'm a bookkeeper at the oil company and I only get time off on the weekends. The week is endless, hopeless. I don't know what the future holds for me or for my son.

When I first saw Will in the emergency room, I wondered if I was to muster the courage to tell him good-bye. The nurse had warned me that this might be our last time together.

But they had already taken him into surgery when I got there that night. Nurse Olson had not been informed; she thought he was still in the emergency room. After we had shuffled down the austere hallway in Section B, and after she checked at the nurse's station, learning that Will was already in the operating room, she ushered me back to the waiting room, trying to reassure me that the doctor would come see me very soon.

Suddenly, I'm back in that stark space, alone. The hospital lobby is stuffy and the air has an undertone of bleach. Wanting to focus on something besides the roar inside my head, I notice that the walls are faded, no longer sanitary white, and are scraped in places from the hundreds of gurneys that have bumped into them. The pictures on the walls are cheap reproductions of rural scenes, and above the double doors are large blue plastic signs announcing the areas of the hospital that lie ahead.

I stumble over to one of the six blue vinyl chairs, attached to each other in a line. Unsure, I sit down stiffly. The thinly padded vinyl seat offers little comfort and the metal arms dig into my forearms. To my right is a battered coffee table with severely outdated magazines scattered on top. The faint buzz of the computer at the nurse's station and what must be a muffled breathing device are the only sounds I hear. It's nearly 4 a.m. and I'm the only person in the waiting area.

I stare down at my hands, twisting and knotting them as if doing so would hold back the turmoil inside me. My hands used to be pretty. Now they lie folded and distorted in my lap as I tread time in the cold waiting room. I look down at them—it's as if they are someone else's hands. My mother's maybe, how I remember her hands so papery thin and fragile as she sat in her chair at the old age home. I see them now, and they are bruised beyond belief. *How is it that old people's skin purples and blobs so easily?*

I look down at my hands again and think: *I will never have the smooth skin of youth again.* Veins bulge blue like rivulets along the lines of my fingers. Knuckles wrinkle with the dehydration of a desert floor cracking under summer sun.

Where did I go? Where is my son? Will we find each other again?

My despair roams the room, is expelled by my breath, and unconsciously I do my best to bite down on the pain that brought me here.

The automatic sliding doors open, startling me. A pair of uneasy parents enters with a small child clutched tightly in the mother's arms. The glass doors whoosh behind them and close. They make their way quickly to the tall counter where the admissions clerk barricades herself. She issues "visitor" tags to the parents, who absently clip them onto a piece of clothing. They are more interested in getting their child in to see the doctor.

"Please wait while I have the orderly meet you at the double doors to escort you to the exam room," she says in her rehearsed voice.

Finally, she pushes the button and the sluggish doors open to allow them to pass through. The orderly waits on the other side, then ushers them down the stark hallway and out of sight.

Alone again, I stand up and cross to the counter to ask the girl if the doctor will be coming out soon. I tell her my son Will was brought in by ambulance around 2 a.m.

She stares blankly at me for a moment then looks down at her clipboard.

"Yes, Ma'am. He was taken into emergency surgery at around 3 a.m., so Doctor Schwimmer should be coming out here to the waiting room to talk to you. I can't tell you when that will be, ma'am."

"Okay," I say, my voice wavering and weak. I feel like an uninvited guest.

I walk back to my designated chair-in-a-line. The walls compress upon me and I whisper to God: *Please let me see my son again; please let him live.*

It must have been a couple of hours later after that

when the girl at the counter announces, "Family of Will Alves?"

I'm still the only human being in the waiting room. She can't even make eye contact with me. She stares blankly at the far wall.

I walk over to the tall counter and stand in front of her.

"I'm Beverly Alves, Will's mother."

"The surgeon will be out to meet with you in ten minutes."

After hours of waiting, those ten minutes dragged on endlessly. I had moved on from hope and expectation to desperate anxiety to an unstoppable stream of tears.

The doctor makes his entrance through the double doors and walks directly to me.

"Mrs. Alves. Your son pulled through the surgery. He's somewhat stable now."

I nearly pass out from relief.

"Can I see him? I have to see my boy."

I'm already pushing past him to make a break for those formidable doors and mysterious hallway beyond.

"Yes, of course. But I have to warn you, he's in rough shape," says Dr. Schwimmer, holding me back by my arms. "Let me get Nurse Olson to take you back to the recovery room."

BEVERLY: ADRIFT

Sons are the anchors of a mother's life.

— Sophocles

As the weeks wore on, I realized Will would be paralyzed the rest of his life. The doctor talked to us one morning on his rounds. He was going to keep Will for about six weeks in traction on the rotating bed with the tongs. But after that, we had to decide where he would have to go.

"Where he has to *go*?" I asked Dr. Schwimmer, the irritation sounding in the tone of my voice. "What does that mean *exactly*?"

"We can't keep him here at the hospital indefinitely. Once he's completed the treatment with the traction, he has to leave. You may want to look into a nursing home. He'll be in a wheelchair from now on," Dr. Schwimmer cooed in his habitual bedside tone of voice.

A sand pit opened up and swallowed me at that moment.

When I was going to see my son twice a week, once on Wednesday nights and once each Sunday, Leon spent all of his time working on the ranch. He wouldn't drive me to Billings; he wouldn't come with me to see Will — this boy who was so mangled, with his black eyes and swollen face. Leon wouldn't even visit when his parents made the token pilgrimage to see Will, to let him know they cared for him.

Maybe Leon thought he was helping us financially by working extra days on the ranch, but he never let me know that. All I thought of was the mound of debt piling up with Will's unpaid medical bills, the ongoing expenses of traveling two hundred miles twice a week, and finding babysitters for little Janie. Most times, Gordy couldn't watch her because he had an after-school job at the Irma Hotel as a bell boy. I begged the mothers of Janie's classmates to take her several weeks in a row when I knew I had to be with my boy.

Funny how a mother is torn and guilty about spending inordinate amounts of time with one child, feeling like we neglect the others, yet loving them all the more for their resilience.

Overwhelmed with the aspects of Will's care and all the ramifications that made on me personally, I panicked at the thought of what to do with Gordy and Janie.

Instinctively, I knew that they would suffer from my

inattention. And, how would Leon and I finance all of this? My folks didn't have the means to help, and neither Leon nor I made very good money. Fossilized by fear, I found myself at a standstill, not moving forward, frozen in place.

My weekly visits with Will continued. Our conversations meandered from the inconsequential to the astounding impacts of the accident. Will knew, intellectually, how serious his injuries were, and that asking Vincent to move him that night finished severing his spinal cord. We didn't go into too much detail about it, though. We didn't tread the ground that would explore the depths of his emotional damage. We carefully avoided all references to hopelessness, despair, and despondence over his condition.

"What happened is done," I told my son. "Nothing can change it. We have to go on and not worry over it too much."

Despite my brave words, the burden of worry settled on me anyway. Endless nights without sleep filled my head about how miserably I was fulfilling my responsibilities to my son. The accident had upped the ante. I'd been thrown into a strange world of police reports, insurance claims, and medical bills pouring in every day. I made dozens of phone calls. I signed reams of paperwork. But that was only half of my worry. Not only were financial unknowns bearing down, constantly on my mind was what was going to happen to Will, to me, and to Gordy and Janie. Would he have to live in a nursing home, if he even survived this? How would I pay for something like that? I tried going to work every day. If I didn't, they would fire me and then I wouldn't have a job either.

The worst of it happened when I'd run into Will's friends, sometimes at the grocery store or gas station.

"Hey, Mrs. Alves. How's Will doing? We miss him, you know." They'd smile but wouldn't look directly at me, and I heard the hesitation in their voices.

The ache would deepen as I looked at them, and for a moment I'd think of all that Will could not be now. But I couldn't sift those experiences and take only the part that didn't hurt. It all blended together in a blur of painful emotion.

"He's doing well," I'd reply, and smile at them. "He'd love to have a visitor. If you can go see him, or write a note; he's pretty lonely right now."

They'd nod and say *for sure, Mrs. Alves, tell Will I'll see him soon.*

More times than not, they wouldn't visit or write to him.

I did not ask for my son to be narrowed down to life in a wheelchair. This was a journey unplanned for both of us. I found myself forced to navigate through a hostile and rough terrain. Worry. Sadness. Fear. Guilt. Helplessness. Anger. Confusion. Disappointment. More Worry.

This painful tangle of emotions set me back; it set us all back. At first, I tried to avoid the sadness and regret. I was angry. All the time. I found out that this is an understandable impulse.

Most of all, I didn't want Will to be perceived as someone who couldn't do the things that any other high school student could do. As I came full circle, having already experienced the denial, anger, guilt, and sadness of those inevitable reactions, I found that I was eventually free to search for information and solutions to the problems we faced. I somewhat transformed my emotions into energy and pushed to get my son a good education. I knew without that, his path would be long and arduous.

I began to conserve my strength and focus on becoming Will's advocate. In some ways, I became an expert in learning all I could about his disabling condition and how that could best be remedied. At some point, I started moving through the mourning of the "loss" of my son and took action.

I had to deal with getting him reinstated in school and the anxiety and pressure rocketed as soon as I scheduled the meeting with the principal and counselor. I pulled into the parking lot with my stomach already in knots. I was completely intimidated. We sat down in the principal's office and they asked me what I thought. I didn't know what to say. And, being speechless was usually not a problem for me.

Finally, I was able explain what the therapists at the

rehab center did to get Will set up for "attending" his classes with the portable speaker system. *Would that be possible here?* I asked, then kicked myself for sounding so meek.

Besides the challenges of keeping Will in school and making sure he had all the choices for his education that the other students had, I had to go to battle to prove his eligibility for benefits and services afforded to those "elite" disabled.

Today, I am going into a hearing with a two-foot-tall stack of reports and notes. I have copies of laws and regulations that are highlighted and dog-eared. I have a very firm resolve that we will leave no stone unturned in seeing that Will gets the appropriate benefits necessary for him to become a happy, competent adult.

I am not going to bang on the table. I am not going to threaten or yell. I am going to calmly listen to what they have to offer Will, and tell them that we will do whatever it takes to see that he receives the education and benefits he is entitled to.

I dare them to deny him. If they do, I will find out who can steer us to someone who can. But, I am no longer nervous and timid.

BEVERLY: CHANGING COURSE

"The pure rage that stems from an unredressed injury can be more fearsome than that produced by the original wrong."
— Gerry Spence, respected
attorney-litigator and commentator
on civil rights in America

I am a Leo, born in the month of August, the month of intense heat and powerful emotions. I was confronted by outside forces that demanded that I change and adapt to new conditions. I resisted. Painfully, at first. I was not one to move easily into new situations unless I was the one to make the first move. This was hoisted upon me, and I responded with a roar.

I'd been given the name of an attorney, someone who advocated for people like us, those of us who didn't have options and were faced with such distressing and unexpected hurdles.

On a Tuesday night, after work, I sat on the couch in his office. My face reddened and my fists clenched as I told him about my son Will and his predicament.

"He's been in an accident; it has left him paralyzed. We can't seem to get any help with his care, and the insurance companies just keep pointing fingers at each other. In the meantime, the bills pour in. I can't keep this up!

"It's complicated, because it was Will's car that they wrecked, and it was his friend who was driving. I don't want Vincent to get in trouble—Will had a hand in the way things happened too. But I cannot see any way to care for my son if we don't have some kind of aid to see this through."

The attorney nodded and reassured me that he would take a thorough look at things. As he sifted through several inches of the documents I'd brought to our meeting, he said, "Mrs. Alves, we have a case that I can defend here."

I couldn't believe what I heard. *Is there hope for my son?* I dared not go down that path until I knew it was real.

"What do we have to do now?" I asked.

"First of all, Mrs. Alves, don't let your emotions be your Achilles' heel in this process. You must trust me, and you must trust the process so that your son can have a reasonable quality of life as a quadriplegic. I have to warn you, this could take some time, a considerable amount of time, to sort out."

"Okay. What should I do in the meantime?" His last statement made me nervous. My son had immediate needs that couldn't wait for a sluggish judicial system to play out.

He said, "I know you are frightened, and you feel helpless and out of control right now. But try not to blame this on the unsympathetic approach of the insurance companies. And don't blame yourself, or God, or bad luck. Just focus on the next step, on what's in front of you at any given moment."

I stared blankly at him. *What?*

"I know a lot of what I'm telling you doesn't make sense right now. That's why we are going to talk once a week until we move through this and get to the end."

"Can you make sure that it is only a fight between those insurance people and not my son and his friend?" I pleaded. I knew Will was as concerned about Vincent's state of mind as he was about who could take over his care while I was at work.

"I can't guarantee that, Mrs. Alves." He had such kind eyes as he said it. "I *can* guarantee that Will won't suffer any more than he already has," and then he stood up, walked around his desk, and embraced me. It was the first human touch I'd experienced in quite a while.

I left the attorney's office that day with hope and desperation. I wanted to believe his words of encouragement, but reality had proved things different these past several months.

There were so many unknowns, so many alarming twists and turns that happened every day. I had no idea how enduring and severe the damage would be, both for my son, for me, and for my other children. I didn't care if it was God, bad luck, or fate.

Would Will be the ultimate loser? Yes, of course.

Could I really regain my trust in God, in a power so great that everything could be set right again? I had no answers. I was bitter. I didn't know why we had been subjected to this horrible fate. *Where would it end?*

BEVERLY:
A SIMPLER TIME AND PLACE

*"We must be willing to let go of the life we have planned,
so as to have the life that is waiting for us."*

— E.M. Forster

I look at my boy these days and the monumental trials he faces every day, and I find myself thinking of my earlier life, when Everett and I first married and started having children. We didn't aspire to great things—we wanted only those basic most satisfying elements—love, family, friends, children, and an adequate livelihood. I yearned for Everett and for those days. We had such hope, such faith that all would unfold as it should. And it did. Just not in the form I'd imagined when I was eighteen years old, graduating as the valedictorian of my class, and marrying my love that same afternoon. We had such fun as a new, married couple, even though we'd been dating for two years and all of our friends and cousins took for granted that we were already a couple.

Everett had enlisted in the US Navy before we married, and came home on furlough for our wedding day. The next day, he left for the Great Lakes Training Center in Chicago. I'd started a new job at the electric company in Montrose, but a few weeks later, Everett wrote to tell me he'd found a place for us to live and please come. I felt guilty telling my new boss that I was quitting after just a few weeks, but once I bought my train ticket and boarded at the station, I had no second thoughts. Everett met me at the train station in Chicago, and well he did. First, we took the subway train, then the "L" train, which was built above the streets. When we got off the L, we walked down the stairs to street level where we caught a trolley car. After the trolley dropped us, we walked four or five blocks to our room. I met Mrs. Ingesson, a Swede, and she was so very nice, probably because she knew that Everett was of the same descent. She ushered us to our room that night, informing me that we had laundry and cooking privileges, which meant she opened her home to us as if we were family. Our room was not very private, though, and we had to be quiet as church mice when we made love after lights out.

We took our meals family style with our landlady in her dining room on the first floor. One night, we started talking about how our parents and grandparents ended up coming to America. It was, after all, 1944, a time when many were immigrating to this country. Mrs. Ingesson took me under her wing after that, and we spent many pleasant evenings together.

After Everett received his honorable discharge, we headed back to Colorado. He and his brother Martin, with their dad's help, began to scratch out a living in those high Colorado meadows, where their sheep grazed and they herded them across Cimarron Creek. The men and the sheep climbed over Cerro Summit in mid-summer where the Tabeguache Utes probably moved through the area centuries ago on their journeys between the Gunnison east of Cimarron. People say that was where the Indians spent their summers. In the fall, they must have migrated on foot over Touch-Me-Not Mountain, to their winter destination in the Uncompahgre Valley to the west.

Everett's dad set us up in a cracker box sized house in the saddle of Cimarron Pass. On cold winter evenings, he'd stop by after checking on the livestock to warm himself. He'd always have a story or two to tell, which entertained me immensely and bored Everett to tears, since he'd heard them dozens of times.

One of his stories was how the cattlemen and sheep men came to tolerate each other. As we sat at the kitchen table near the warm stove, he talked about the mining boom and as it fell off, ranching took over in Cimarron country. Both sheep and cattle were run in the open lands of the Cimarron Valley and the hills nearby. Cimarron became a major livestock shipping center, with corrals covering massive amounts of land next to the railroad siding. Local ranchers would drive their stock to Cimarron and time their arrival to allow on the spot loading of animals, as there was no way to feed the livestock at the corrals. They shipped them mostly in the spring and fall and then moving the animals to a winter range in the desert areas around Grand Junction, Colorado, or into Utah.

I was content and happy with my role as mother and homemaker, side by side with Everett as we planned our future together.

Everett and his brother Martin pressed on, building up their stock and enjoying their time together. They walked the upper meadows every summer, sleeping on the ground, and tending the herds until it was time to drive the stock to Cimarron Valley.

One spring, because of our expanding family, Everett took on a second job. He got hired on with a construction crew who was tearing out an old railroad line that ran through the San Juan Mountains.

BEVERLY: LOSING STREAK

All-in: A bet that places all of a player's chips into the pot.

— Dictionary of Poker Terms

Late evening, and still no Everett. The fresh-picked asparagus now lay limp, lifeless, and a sickly yellow-green in the bottom of the casserole dish. By now, my sons, who earlier were freshly bathed and dressed in their Sunday best matching cowboy shirts, sported tousled hair and untucked tails. They chased each other about the house, yelling and wrestling each other to the floor.

"Boys, quiet! Sit down! We aren't leaving without Daddy, so hush up, all of you!" Frazzled myself, I debated whether to call the neighbors and try to catch a ride to town without him.

"I'm hungry, Mom," Will whined, gazing up at me. Absently, I reached down and softly swept my hand across his chubby face.

Sucking on his thumb, Gordy clung to my leg, whimpering and nodding in agreement with his brother.

"We'll eat soon, boys. Daddy will be home any minute."

As if on cue, tires ground to a halt on the gravel driveway outside.

"See? That's him right now!" I rushed to the window and peered out into the dusk, expecting to see Everett's faded blue pickup. Instead, I spotted my mom and dad's sedan, dust billowing behind the wheels. I cracked the screen door, then walked onto the porch and waved. The boys followed.

"Hold up, now," I cautioned them. "Don't get yourselves dirty by going outside."

"It's Grandpa and Grandma!" Will yelled, hoping for the surreptitious snack that usually accompanied their visits. He leaned around the side of my legs to watch them.

My dad slowly emerged from the familiar pastel yellow Chevy, then shuffled over to Mom's side of the car. He opened the door for her, guiding her gently from the recesses of the shadowy interior. He linked his arm in hers and turned toward the house. Both heads bowed, they seemed to study the barren gravel at their feet.

"Mom? Dad? What happened? What's wrong?" I could hear the strain my voice. I knew something bad was going on.

They didn't answer. Wearily climbing the steps, Mom leaned on Dad for support.

Just as they reached the top step of the porch, Gordy shoved from behind and Will bumped against my legs.

"Gordy, stop it! Mom, he's pushing me!"

"Boys, go inside," my dad quietly commanded, looking directly at the boys.

"C'mon, let's go in," Dean cajoled the little boys, putting his arm around Gordy and leading him into the house. Will lingered; he must have seen that Mom could barely stand. Her sobs were lost in Dad's shirt sleeve as she buried her head into the crook of his arm.

"Oh, my God, what is it?" I stumbled back against the screen door.

Daddy said, "Hell, honey, there's no easy way to say it. Everett is dead."

WILL: STEPDADS

If you cannot get rid of the family skeleton,
you may as well make it dance.

— George Bernard Shaw

Who among us hasn't wished for different cards to play? *He* deals and we end up with a crappy hand. So, we try throwing in a few cards to get better ones on the second draw. That works, sometimes. Other times, not so much. Some of us think of a strategy to use the hand we're dealt—maybe we bluff our way through it— but ultimately, that backfires too. Others just fold and check out of the game right away. That's what my dad did—he folded with a losing hand, at age twenty-eight, and that was it.

After the construction accident, life for all of us—me, Gordy, Dean, and my mom—changed dramatically. Faced with raising three small sons on her own, Mom was determined to carry on what she and Dad wanted for us boys—she wanted to raise us in the manner they had talked about so many times, the two of them sitting at the kitchen table, planning the things they wanted to teach us and how they wanted to teach us. That meant we boys needed a father to help carry out these plans. So, Mom married again. And again. And again.

I was very young when she married Stepfather Number One, but I remember him. Hector, who I later labeled SF #1, considered stepchildren an annoyance and hindrance to his desire to sit on the sofa and drink whiskey. We were typical boys, and we were energetic. I'm the middle brother and was maybe five or six at the time; Gordy was around four, and Dean was two years older than I was. As any boys that age, we were boisterous, loud, and clumsy, playing underfoot while Mom cooked dinner. At any random moment, any of us three boys would cause an eruption.

"You little shits! Stop your running around." He'd spit the words at us, eyes gleaming and out of focus. "Shut your traps and sit down before I take my belt to you."

He was a mean drunk who whipped us boys more often than not to "teach us a lesson." The lessons learned: Stay out of his line of fire when he got home at night; don't make any noise; and don't bring attention to yourself.

The three of us eventually devised a system of deflection that we used on a regular basis. If one of us was the target of his wrath, the other two created a distraction. Then, when his attention turned to them, the first one would hightail it to Mom to warn her as to what was coming. Most times, she'd run interference for us and take the brunt of his brutality.

Before we learned this system, however, there were plenty of mishaps. Like the time he brought some of his personal things out of storage and decorated the house. One such item was a small, framed photograph. He'd set it on the end table by the sofa, and one day I picked it up and studied it closely. The picture was of a stringy-haired woman standing in front of a row of wooden shacks. There were a few dirty-faced kids in front of her, and she had a firm grip on them with her man-sized hands.

Everything about her, from the lack of an expression on her face to the way she restrained the children, felt bitter and uninviting. I was six years old and whatever I thought at the time just came right out of my mouth.

"Why does this lady look so mean?" I asked no one in particular; I thought I was alone, and I was simply talking to myself. But Hector, who'd been unloading beer into the ice box, heard me.

He roared out of the kitchen in his drunken fury and screamed at me, "That's my mother, you little bastard! Don't you *ever* talk shit about her again, *you hear me*?!"

I tried to melt into the back of the sofa, afraid to breathe or move.

With each failed marriage, Mom determined that a

change of scenery was in order. My little sister, Janie, was only six months old when Mom left Hector. We packed up and headed out from Naturita, a small, insignificant bump in the southern Colorado Desert, to Walden at the northernmost corner of the state. The ill-fated union with the dreadful SF #1 was over.

When we arrived in Walden in May of 1960, I was eleven years old and ready to get back to farm living, the kind we were used to before Hector turned our lives upside down. My brothers and I survived the "tests" the other kids dished out once we were marked as the "new kids" in town. We proved that we could beat the status quo, which made friends of some and enemies of others. School let out shortly after we moved to Walden, so we either roamed the surrounding area, or went with our new stepfather on his brand inspecting rounds. We met a lot of ranchers and their kids, which helped a lot before being thrown back into school in the fall.

I started in sixth grade at Walden, an instant hit on the basketball court. I stood at least three inches above all the boys in my age group, and stood eye to eye with most of the eighth graders. I was a tank, so establishing my position or standing in a game was a breeze—except for the seventh and eighth graders, who insisted on bullying me around. I didn't push back, didn't know about fighting, backing down at the first sign of power plays. I didn't know my own strength when it came to standing up for myself with the older boys. But I did use my size and strength to help win in team sports, especially basketball. That's when I formed friendships and began to feel respected by the other boys.

Our junior high basketball team had a complex structure. Varsity was made up of seventh and eighth graders and maybe a stand-out seventh grader. Then the rest of the boys in sixth and seventh grade (including me) made up the Junior Varsity team. Because of my height and muscle, I won the position as starting center. I'd not played much basketball before that, but I finally managed to learn the strategy and contribute to the team. I was "in" by then, and part of the group of boys who always hung around together.

We started pulling pranks, like stealing pop bottles from behind the general store and selling them back for movie and popcorn money. Then we'd sneak into the adult movies. We'd heard about the popular one with the on-stage stripper when we overheard a couple of our dads shooting the breeze. We wanted to see skin and sex (or as much as we knew about it at that point).

What I really loved was marbles, our daily sport on the school grounds every morning and after school. My shooter style was fast and flat, but that didn't help me shoot well. Our playing field was lumpy dirt, not rolled smooth, so my shooter bounced over opponents' marbles, giving me grief. As disgraceful as I was on the playground, I did manage to win the North Park tournament, and place second in the district during seventh and eighth grade.

So, the fall was marbles and basketball, plus deer hunting. By then I had a .22 rifle for expeditions with my brothers and friends.

I also learned to fish on the Michigan and Illinois Rivers, two of the county's blue ribbon trout streams.

Adolescence was rushing into my veins at age twelve. I'd been going to a church youth group, where interaction with girls tormented me.

I'd see Sharon there every Wednesday after school.

"Hi, Will," she'd greet me with her smooth, delicate voice.

My face heated up; my palms began to sweat.

"Hey, Sharon," I'd say, turning away so I wouldn't have to say more.

But she'd sit down by me, sometimes touching my hand when we played board games. Sharon was my last thought at night when I shut out my light.

Then *Playboy* began to replace the car magazines. When I helped Mom at the Laundromat, I'd zero in on the *Ladies' Home Journal* articles about breast-feeding. I bored my friends with talk about how "Sharon is so pretty," and "She tells me funny jokes."

Somewhere along the way, probably while out at the honky-tonk for dances, Mom met Gary Nichols, the county brand inspector. Eventually, they married, and he became SF #2. But I got along with Gary just fine. He taught Gordy and me to hunt rabbits, which we did with a vengeance, because he would pay us a quarter for each one we brought back to him. There was a big steel bin in back of the lumber yard that we tossed the dead bunnies into—I'm not sure who skinned them for the fur, or what they did with those furless remains. All I knew was that my pockets were always heavy with change. For most of my junior high school days, we lived in Walden. I made friends with some of the other boys my age. I was happy there.

When Mom's marriage to SF #2 blew apart, we moved again. As if exiled, we trudged south, this time to Greeley, one of those dirt-poor, hardscrabble Colorado towns full of migrant field workers and their kids.

That's when the future SF #3—Leon Langdon—roared into our lives. We knew Mom had been seeing someone— she loved to date and dance—but we weren't too concerned about it until she wanted us to meet him. We were to go to lunch on a Sunday over at Randy's South Side diner. This rendezvous meant she might be getting serious with this character. As we walked into the café, my first look at Leon raised the hair on my neck. My heartbeat rattled in my rib cage.

Leon Langdon was a large, dark man. Under a black wide-brimmed cowboy hat, his brows furrowed into a permanent frown. His face was a swarthy leather-brown, deeper than just years outside in the sun. His chambray shirt pulled taut on his arms, which bulged with muscle. Below his canvas vest, a leather-sheaved knife hung at his side. His dusty boots, with their two-inch heels, proved he'd been cow punching for many seasons.

"You must be Will." He stepped toward me, his gristly hand extended. "How are you, boy?" His booming drawl made "boy" sound like "bo-ah." I forced myself to look up from his boots and shook his hand, trying to match the force of his grip. His walnut eyes punctured my coolness—I couldn't hold his gaze and I looked away, catching my breath.

We suffered the interminable lunch with Mom's new beau. We couldn't get out of that diner fast enough. But some of his comments had piqued my curiosity. Afterward, I asked Mom a bunch of questions. He'd told us that he'd been a corporal in the Army and was stationed at Fort Hood, Texas for most of his military career. He claimed he boxed as a Golden Glove contender after being honorably discharged in '61. He told Mom he didn't really see a future in professional boxing, so he went to work on ranches—cow punching and branding, breaking horses, and such.

"Mom, why is his skin so dark? Is he Mexican?" I asked her, while we were sitting in the living room, watching our Sunday night shows.

"No, he's not. His family came from Morocco," she said.

"What? Where's that?" I'd heard of it before, but couldn't dredge up my geography lessons enough to place where in the world Morocco was.

"It's somewhere over by Arabia," Mom said. "Leon told me that his great-grandparents immigrated to America to get away from the persecution over their Christian beliefs."

"Wow! That must've been tough for them." I was more impressed with my version of his ancestors, picturing them wrapped in turbans and spurring their ponies across the sand dunes to reach their freedom ship.

Leon started showing up at our house every Saturday night for dinner. The months went on. Gordy and I went to school in Greeley and got into lots of fistfights that year. I broke my leg, too, and was in a body cast for what seemed like forever. Sometime that winter, after I got my cast off, Leon started teaching me to box. He knew about the fistfights and how tough those local kids could be, so he wanted to give me an advantage over them.

He told me that he'd been a Golden Gloves boxer in the Army, so I asked him one dreary rain-soaked afternoon if he would teach me some stuff. Leon dug out a pair of sixteen-ounce gloves that he'd seen in a crate on the back porch at the ranch he was working at. Then he rigged up sparring mitts by filling an oversized pair of leather mittens with the stuffing from an old pillow that Mom gave us.

When we got our boxing "ring" set up in the garage, Leon told me, "We need to start with the basics, so I'm going to show you the boxing stance first." He helped me lace up my gloves. Angling his feet a little wider than his shoulders, he showed me how to keep my weight even across both legs and keep my knees bent.

"Elbows down, hands up like this." He motioned to me to move in closer. "Now, watch what I do," he said, jabbing toward my chest with his left and snapping a straight punch with his right, barely grazing my cheek.

Startled, I stepped backward. He stepped forward, keeping the distance short between us.

"Did you know that boxing is called the 'sweet science'?" asked Leon.

I shook my head, keeping an eye on his right fist.

"And did you know that the jab is actually the most important punch in boxing? Because it'll get you *into* trouble and it'll get you *out* of trouble."

I pulled the boxing gloves on, tying up the strings on the right glove while Leon helped me with the left. Then Leon donned the sparring mitts, holding them in place by wrapping electrical tape around one wrist and me clumsily wrapping the tape around the other.

"Okay, now it's your turn to try the jab. Rotate your hand palm down when you extend from the neutral position—that's it—and you'll see how that will give you torque and power."

I poked gingerly at him, standing sideways and stiff as a board.

"Now, this time, turn your hips towards me as you start the jab and lean forward."

Leon held the mitt in position and had me repeat my

jabs about a dozen times. My thrust was slow and soft, so we switched gloves and he showed me his technique.

"The basic jab is like a piston. It fires out and recoils back to guard position. It has to have lightning speed; if it doesn't, you're going to get hit a lot. Another thing: Keep your chin tucked behind your shoulder."

After a few more jabs, he wanted to show me move number two, the straight punch.

"This one comes from your rear hand, and it's way more powerful than the jab. But it's the same as the jab — your hand goes from neutral in guard position to palm down at extension."

He showed me a couple of straights, then he added, "Now for the footwork. Think of your rear foot as squashing a bug." He twisted his foot inward, shifting his weight from back to front to transfer the power of the punch. "Don't forget to rotate the shoulders again. Keep your hand high and throw it in a straight line to your target. Then keep it on the same path to return to guard position, here by your head."

After that first lesson, he decided we needed a speed bag—first, to help figure out my dominant hand, and second, to help me fine-tune my reaction time. I was kind of scrawny at that point, so the workouts would build my arm and shoulder strength.

I was in good with the shop teacher at the Greeley High School, so I called Mr. Hayek to see if he'd let us use wood scraps, the saws, drills, and welder to fashion a speed bag platform and brackets. I convinced Mom to sew the speed bag for us out of an old canvas water bag Leon found in the barn at the ranch. We filled it with clean sand, sealed it, and attached it with a heavy-duty swivel we bought at the hardware store. We bolted the bracket to the far wall in the garage near our boxing ring area.

The first time we used it, he watched me as I hit the bag ten times with my left, then ten times with my right; then he had me switch back and forth until he could see that my right made better circles and didn't tire as fast.

"Now we know which one is your dominant hand," he told me.

"What does that mean? Do I lead my punches with it?"

"No, it belongs in the back. Your dominant hand has all the power. Use your left to measure your range and set up for the punch. Then your back hand — your right — carries the power, like a cannon — POW!"

He jabbed his left toward my chest, then shot a right to my chin, stopping just before impact.

We'd go at it for hours at a time, Leon showing me the boxing moves that he'd learned in the military boxing rings.

In the spring, Mom and Leon got hitched. Then, he landed a ranch job in Wyoming. Plans were made, once again, to drag us from our home. We followed Leon north to the heart of Buffalo Bill country and settled in Cody. Gordy and I were glad to get out of Greeley, though. That was one tough town, and we hoped it would be the end of the brawls we had put up with week after week.

BEVERLY: HUSBAND II

Three rings of marriage are the engagement ring,
the wedding ring, and the suffering.

— Author Unknown

How does a woman recover from the death of her husband? How did I do it? I cannot remember those days and weeks after the accident. I only remember the endless sleepless nights, missing him, worrying how I was going to care for our boys, falling into deep despair and when the sun came up, more despair.

Mechanically, I moved through the motions of being a young widow with small children. My parents took us under their wing and waited until time could heal me.

I took to having conversations with Everett.

May 21, 1953: *"How could you be gone? We're not done yet, we have our sons to raise. I want to have more children with you. I want a girl. We weren't finished, Everett. Now, I have to finish without you."*

The next week it was dismal and raining when I went to his grave.

"How can I live here without you? I just want this pain to end. If it ends, is that the end of you? Will I forget your warm arms around me? Will I forget your face, your kind eyes?"

June 26, 1953: *"You know how much I hate being alone. How can I go on without you? You know me better than anyone, Everett. I need you here with me."*

July 13, 1953: *"How could you leave me now, just when we were really getting to know each other?"*

October 1, 1953: *"It's so hard to be in love with a dead man."*

November 30, 1953: *"I'm homeless. Widowhood did this to me. I still eat and sleep here, but it is not home to me."*

February 5, 1954: *"I woke this morning remembering the dream of us, thinking, 'This is too good to be true.' Then, I wonder, where to from here? You are gone. I have to make my way alone."*

Eventually, I did make my way back to the "normal" life of a widowed woman in the days when being single wasn't the best standing to find oneself in.

My cousins Velda and Richard invited me to a barn dance a few miles down the road in Shavano Valley. They said they wanted me to meet Richard's cousin, Hector, a nice man close to my age. Flatly, I agreed. I had no interest in anyone. But it was convenient because my folks lived next door; they said they would watch the boys.

And I hadn't been to a dance in nearly two years.

I barely remember the evening, but I do remember the moment I met Hector. He was definitely related to Richard: tall and charming, even funny with his witticisms about the other dancers. We started dating, and within six months, we married.

By next March, my baby girl was born. I visited Everett at the cemetery and told him what a gift she was, that I thought he would be happy, too, that I finally had our girl after bearing all those boys.

I was committed to being a good wife; I did not regret marrying Hector. Until he started in on my boys. Maybe he felt pressured to be the man of the house, with so many "mouths to feed," especially with the new baby, Janie. I don't know what sent him into orbit, but it wasn't good. I believed in discipline, and it didn't bother me that he got after the boys for misbehaving. But when he started pulling his belt off and chasing them, pressing them down to the floor, and flailing that belt on them, I came unglued. They were so little, just young tykes. This was too much for me.

The baby was six months old when I packed us up and left. We stayed with my folks in Shavano Valley while I got back on my feet. I took a temporary job at the Montrose County Courthouse, selling license plates.

BEVERLY: NORTH PARKERS

Bride, n. A woman with a fine prospect behind her.
— Ambrose Bierce,
The Devil's Dictionary, 1911

Moving to Walden was the best choice I'd made in quite some time. The small town is in the center of a large open valley called North Park, high in the northern Colorado Rockies. The town residents call themselves "North Parkers." As we settled in to life there, the community welcomed us and we became "North Parkers," too. The boys were happy, they had friends, and they did well in school. They played sports and life seemed to balance out for a while.

I met Gary Nichols, the county brand inspector, in the fall when all of us parents were going to the high school football games. We found out we had a lot in common — we both loved to square dance, and he wanted a family as much as I did. After dating for eight or nine months, we thought it would be a good idea to provide a solid father figure for the boys and Janie, so we married. We went into business for ourselves. Gary was tired of the travel for brand inspecting, so he bought the local lumber yard. I became his bookkeeper. We went along like this for quite a while. Then I found out he still had a woman on the side in Coalmont, a small town about a half hour from Walden.

I confronted him.

"Gary, I know that you're seeing another woman over in Coalmont," I said to him one night after the kids were in bed. I didn't want them to hear the conversation. "What is going on?"

"I don't know what you're talking about, Bev. Why would I do that?"

"You tell me. Because I got it on good standing that is what's happening," I fumed at him, pacing back and forth to the kitchen sink and back to the table. I couldn't sit down. I leaned on my hands, getting close to his face.

"Can you tell me right now that you're not seeing someone else?"

He looked away, sighed, and slumped in his chair.

"Okay, Bev. You're right. It's too much for me, with all these kids in the house, and I'm not doing so well at the lumber yard. I don't know what else to say." He bent his head into his chest and wouldn't look up.

I went to the courthouse the next day and filed for divorce.

BEVERLY: GREELEY, COLORADO

*Don't be discouraged. It's often the last
key in the bunch that opens the lock.*

— Unknown

Moving to Greeley seemed reasonable to me at the time. I would be closer to my folks, but not back in my hometown, where the gossip would be too much for me. I got a bookkeeper job right away at JC Penney Company there in Greeley, settling in and getting the kids enrolled in school. Dean had already graduated in Walden, enlisted in the Air Force, and was stationed in Bangor, Maine. Will and Gordy were reluctant to leave Walden; they loved it there and had made many close friends. Guilt set in when I realized they were once again being uprooted and forced to adapt to a new place, a new school, and being treated like outsiders. Janie was young, I wasn't as concerned about her, but one day shortly after we moved there, she came running into the house, upset and crying.

"What's the matter, my girl?" She'd been next door visiting our elderly neighbor, Mrs. Stillman, who had befriended me the day we moved in.

"She," Janie gasped, out of breath. "She—called me a *spic!*"

We had a talk and I tried to explain that Mrs. Stillman didn't mean anything by it; she just thought that with Janie's dark olive skin and summer tan, she must be part Hispanic.

"But I'm not, Mom," she said, still sniffling and pouting, buried into the sofa. "Why did she say something so mean?"

This should have been a signal to me that my children were facing a harsh and dangerous year in this town filled with children who had to live with the motto "the toughest survive."

The boys found themselves in weekly fistfights, and Janie battled two second-grade boys who would corner her after school and kick her with their hard-soled wingtips.

I woke one night at 2 a.m. to the snap of the doorknob unlocking at the front door. It echoed across the living room and down the hallway to my room. Mrs. Harrison had called me at 12:30 a.m., claiming that her son, Tommy, had been badly beaten up by Will. I didn't know what to do. Should I get Gordy and Janie up and go to her house? She'd hung up on me. I didn't know if she was even home. Did she take Tommy to the emergency room?

I decided to wait until Will came home. When I heard the front door open, I got up and put my robe on. I walked down the hall to Will's room, but before I could knock, I heard him:

"Until you get home, Dean, I'll kill the next bastard that says anything bad about you!"

I opened the door and walked in. Will sat at the end of his bed, clutching a photo of Dean in his Air Force blues.

"Will? Are you all right?" I noticed his swollen lower lip and blood on his right eyebrow. "You didn't mean that, did you? About killing someone?"

Will looked at his brother's photo, then looked up at me.

"God, Mom. I don't know," he said. "Ever since we got word of Dean's plane going down, all the scum in town have been saying things about him."

Will turned and waved the photo at me. "I guess you haven't heard about the petition that's keeping all the draft dodging mommy's boys in this town from going into service, have you?"

Of course, I hadn't heard.

"It's all about defending my brother's honor," he said. "Those SOBs that are getting out of the draft are laughing and celebrating his being shot down because they don't have to go fight now."

I asked Will then, "What did Tommy Harrison have to do with you getting into this situation?"

Will's face turned white. "It's a long story, Mom."

I'd led him into the kitchen by then, and handed him an ice pack.

"Tell me about it. And it better be good."

"Tommy started spouting off about my brother being so scared when the 'Cong got a hold of him that he even cried. That set everybody around him laughing and chiming in. I heard Denson flapping his jaws, too. Then I exploded and took him down."

"What did Tommy have to do with all of this?"

"After the security guard came over to help Denson, Tommy came up to me and started apologizing for what he'd said. That's when I laid into him, too."

I remembered Mrs. Harrison's call.

"We have to get this settled. I'm going to call the Harrisons."

After a lengthy and escalated phone conversation, the Harrisons agreed that Will was justified in reacting the way he did, acknowledging that everyone was on edge these days with the Viet Nam War. They finally told me that they decided not to press charges against Will.

When I turned back to Will, I started sobbing. The stress of this night broke me. I was done.

Will tossed the ice pack on the table and took me in his arms. He pressed me against his chest and said, "Oh, Mom, I'm sorry I caused you so much pain. I don't know what to do."

"Son, you did what you had to do. Your brother couldn't defend himself, so you did it for him. Now, you know that sometimes those things come with a price. But the price is worth it when you do the right thing."

I knew at that moment we had to get out of that place and back "home," wherever that was.

BEVERLY: HUSBAND IV

*Marriage has no guarantees. If that's what you're
looking for, go live with a car battery.*

— Erma Bombeck

I loved Leon. He was good to me, and he was good to my kids. He really liked the boys and Janie, too. He just never figured out that commitment was part of the equation. He tried to be a good stepdad, though.

After we moved to Cody, he and Will were both work-ing on the South Fork. Will was working on one ranch and Leon on another one a few miles down the road. So, he'd stop and pick up Will on the way back home to have supper with us, to try to have family time together. One morning Leon got up to go back out to the ranch and Will went with him, of course.

When they were driving, Leon said to Will, "I didn't know that cars could *make* gas. And this windshield was sure dirty when we came to town last night, but it's nice and clean this morning!"

That's all that was said, and they went out to work on their respective ranches that day. The next night, as usual, they came back into town. Sitting at the supper table, Leon got Will to confess that he'd made a key for the car, and that he and Gordy would climb out on the roof of the porch late at night, hop in the car, and go run around town. Well, I never checked the mileage or how much gas I had in the car. I just didn't think anything about it. Leon caught on and busted them. It was really good for Will. It taught him a good lesson.

But Leon and I had our moments. One night we'd been out dancing and got home late. We were eating some bread and milk or something, and sitting at the kitchen table, talking. I knew that some woman had been chasing him. In fact, she was at the dance hall that night. He was getting pretty close to her. I could see that things were getting that way, so I asked him about it. He just reached over and slapped me on the cheek with the back of his hand. I picked up my glass of milk and was going to throw the milk on him. The glass slipped and broke, hitting him on the bridge of his nose and cutting him open. He bled all over the place and we scrambled to get him patched up.

He told me later, "I'll never forget you because I will always see that scar on my nose when I look in the mirror!" It was kind of funny. But he never messed with me after that, and as far as I know, he broke it off with that woman.

Yes, Leon was good to us in his way, and he tried to do the right things. He just was never there enough. Sure, when it was convenient for him, he was there. But the minute things changed, when Will got into the accident, it sent Leon for a loop. He couldn't handle having an invalid for a stepson. He kept spending more and more time on the ranch, and eventually, he only came into town to see us on Sundays.

Things fell apart fast for us then. I had to focus on Will's care, on getting him situated, so all my attention was on my son. Leon didn't like that at all—he wanted all of my attention. He'd mope around the house on Sundays, making snide comments and trying to convince me to go downtown with him to the bar.

I couldn't leave the house—there were too many things to do every night for Will, and by the time I fell into bed, I was exhausted.

Years later, when I went to visit Leon in Arizona, he took me to see a place. He said he would buy it for us if I would come back to him. I couldn't trust him enough to know that I wouldn't be trapped with the house payments or expenses if something had to be repaired. He wouldn't be there to do those things. And I didn't want to get stuck out in the country by myself.

Even with all the missteps and circumstances that tore us apart, I still missed Leon. A song would play on the radio when I was driving to work. Hank Williams, maybe. Something about love found and love lost. The usual country song, but it tugged at my heart, made me yearn for his arms around me. I'd wake up late at night, usually around 3 a.m., and he would be my first thought. The image of Leon and me, twirling around the dance floor at the bar, or the barn dance over at a ranch on the South Fork, would light up vividly in my mind's eye.

WILL: BEST FRIENDS

You and I are more than friends. We're like a really small gang.

— Unknown

When we moved to Cody in the summer of 1964, Leon helped me get on right away as a hand at the X-L Ranch. So, for a couple of months, I thought I was hot stuff. *Big! Strong! Handsome! Aggressive! Employed!* I didn't get to know many guys my age, but I did have a lot of fun getting acquainted with the girls—about a dozen by my count. Some of the older girls were in their twenties, the high school girls' big sisters, and word got around that I was marrying material. Those schoolgirls were taken by surprise when I walked into Cody High as a junior.

Fall at the school was busy with sports starting up, homecoming, and painting the big "C" on the hill. One of the first guys I met was Vincent Barrett—we found ourselves in a few of the same classes, and we hit it off from the start. Vincent is as much of a smart-aleck as I am, maybe more of one. We started hanging out together, and almost every day after school we had plans to do something.

Football had just ended and we were waiting until wrestling would start up in the winter. In the meantime, our favorite pastime was deer hunting. Before the season opened, we spent a couple of weeks glassing some areas south of town every day after school. We'd spotted several whitetails along the hogback ridges that anchored Rattlesnake Peak.

Vincent and I met up at 4:00 a.m. on opening day. Our plan was to hike past Garland Flats and up into Rattlesnake Mountain. That meant climbing over some irregular sandstone hills separated by wide valleys and then an elevation climb to about sixty-seven hundred feet.

After shutting off the engine, I jumped out of the old pickup I borrowed from my boss at the ranch. I let the tailgate down and pulled on my backpack. I picked up my stepfather's .270 Winchester rifle with iron sights and was greeted by cold metal on bare hands. I slung my weapon over my shoulder and prepared for the long hike. I glanced at Vincent and he looked ready to head out too.

Wordless, we marched over the massive red sandy shale scattered with slabs of limestone. Once we crossed this area, we got into some pinions and small pine trees. Some of the pines had been uprooted by a recent windstorm, slowing us as we picked our way through them.

It was getting close to dawn, legal shooting time, so Vincent and I split up. He went high along the ridge and I walked the valley floor. The sun hit the crest of the hill, but below me shadows still obscured my sight. I noticed how the day's first breezes combed the needles in the pines, causing ripples of light and shadow, tattooing the tree trunks. Puffs of my breath hung in front of me when I exhaled. Every nerve in my body sprang to attention, amplifying sounds and movement. My eyes reached into my surroundings like fingers, penetrating deep into tangled branches, sliding over rocks and around stumps, feeling for the slenderest hint of hidden heartbeats. In the places too deeply shadowed to see anything, my ears roved at will, returning with the report of a branch cracking at the bottom of a ravine, or the snuffling breath of a buck.

I sat down with my back against a sandstone boulder to give Vincent a chance to get into position. I rested the rifle across my thighs and as I sat, the valley came to life. A few birds and bugs flitted around me. A wooly worm bobbled along in the dirt. The whoosh of my breathing magnified in my ears. I tried slowing my breath to silence it. Anxious, I searched for any sign of deer. I tuned my senses in to the frequencies of the wild world surrounding me, occupying every quadrant in my brain. It occurred to me that my mental state is a lot like getting high on pot: heightened senses but my focus narrowing intently on some fascinating minutia. I looked to my left over the top of the boulder. I saw nothing, so I drilled into the shadowy thickness about thirty yards ahead of me.

Walking straight at me was a pair of large antlers and underneath them was the buck's silhouette. I got a five-second snapshot before he disappeared behind a large pile of downfall. I estimated that he'd come into view to the right of the heap of pine branches. I cocked the hammer of my rifle and raised it to eye level, lining up the sights. I waited. No buck. I lowered the rifle and looked to the left of the mound. No buck. A crackle caused me to turn around. I don't know how he did it, but his tail flicked once, taunting me, as he vanished into the underbrush.

Then I heard Vincent whistle. I shouldered the borrowed rifle, a basic pump-action, and turned to walk further into the valley. The plan was for me to drive the animals to Vincent so he could get the first shot. He would have a clear line of sight on any quarry I flushed out of the woods below him. Then we were going to switch so that I could hike the ridge and try to get my deer. The broad, flat meadow would expose me, so I skirted the edge to get some cover through the low scrub and sagebrush. We had only about another hour before the sun would warm the valley floor and compel our prey to go into hiding.

In another instant, a good-sized buck materialized in front of me, frozen in place. His head raised, he smelled the air for danger but didn't detect my scent. Forgetting the plan, heart racing, I slipped the rifle off my shoulder and took aim. Here was my longed-for encounter and I didn't want to blow it. I slid the safety off and squeezed the trigger. Dust exploded at the buck's feet and he bolted forward twenty yards. *Dammit!* I had forgotten that Leon doesn't site his rifle and I didn't adjust my aim. I cussed him again. *Shit. Really?* I have to account for the fact that it is three inches lower than where I want the bullet to hit. I pumped the lever action, and a bullet dropped into the chamber. More deer appeared with the buck. Shaking, I pumped bullets as fast as I could shoot. Booms and echoes bounced off the mountain's walls, causing the deer to mill around. They stayed within shooting range.

Uphill about a hundred yards, Vincent started shooting too. We both had buck fever by then and randomly popped off a string of shots. The deer had finally had enough of the noise and ran off through thick deadfall. Incredibly, a whitetail lay on the ground. Vincent ran down the hill to check out the kill. Less than a yard from the animal, he touched it with the tip of his rifle. No movement. Vincent knelt beside the magnificent, motionless animal.

"Looks like about a twenty-inch spread," Vincent said almost reverently, holding the deer by its antlers. The "forky," a two-point with eye guards, was nowhere near that big of a spread, but I didn't argue with him; I let him bask in his glory.

As much as the buck fever had swept over me minutes ago, my stomach rolled as I thought of the dreaded encounter that ended with a dead creature on the ground. In our macho conceit, we're led to believe that killing an animal constitutes a gesture of respect. It doesn't. It all goes back to showing the world that, as a man, I'm worthy and have proven myself in the eyes of all those hard-bitten, big-bearded outdoorsmen who've gone before me.

"Now the work begins," said Vincent, taking his knife out of its sheath. "We start with breaking the pelvic bone, right?"

Neither of us had much experience with field dressing a deer, but I'd watched my stepdad Gary dozens of times.

"Give me your knife," I said, "and I'll show you how SF #2 used to do this."

I went through the sequence in my head: *Sex organs and rectum are first. Make small, circular cuts and watch that I don't puncture the intestines. Then a small cut through the hide and membrane. Lift and spread with two fingers as I run the knife from crotch to sternum. Open the cavity, remove the bladder. Careful not to let it leak on the meat. Cut the windpipe up high and pull it free. Now the fun starts. Reach elbow-deep into the cavity and roll the innards out and away from the deer. Then cut through the center of the pelvic bone. Good thing*

Leon reminded me to bring the hatchet for this. Cut the skin around the bung-hole and pull the colon out of the body cavity.

"Let's roll him over and I'll have you hold his back legs," I said.

We found the entry spot from the bullet — a clean shot right behind the left shoulder, inside the kill zone, and through the heart and lungs.

"You nailed him!" I was impressed even though I knew we were both simply taking pot shots at the critters.

"Get my canteen, will you?" I asked Vincent. I remembered that SF #2 always had fresh water to rinse the cavity and his bloody hands when he was done. The buck was stiffening by now, a good sign that we should start the field dressing process.

"This poor bastard. I sure hate cutting his balls off," I said as I dropped onto my knees. I took my time. I didn't want to make a dumb mistake, and I wasn't totally sure what I was doing in the first place. A half hour later, I stood up and admired my handiwork.

"I'm going to call you John Colter from now on," said Vincent. I heard the reverence in his voice.

"That's right. I'm a bad-ass mountain man," I said, grinning at my best friend.

We were almost six miles from the truck. Dragging it over the shaley ground would chew the fur right off the thing. So we decided to hack it in two and haul a half on our backs. I heaved the animal onto Vincent's neck, draping legs over each of his shoulders to balance the load. We had some straps and rope, so I tied it to him. Then I kneeled on the ground and slung my half onto my shoulders. I held the legs tight around my neck and stood up. Vincent used the last length of our rope to secure it.

We started hiking and hoped there were no other hunters out and about. They might mistake us for trophies instead of humans. Trying to ignore the fact that a bloody deer carcass was riding piggyback on us, we relived the day's adventures. We argued over who was the most feverish in our wild volley of shots with no thought of taking serious aim at our targets; we praised each other for our tenacity until the quarry dropped dead. The report took shape as we marched along, composing the details of our prowess, how we outwitted the animals, and nailing down the precise distance of the shot that took the buck down. We carefully repackaged the moments of truth, firming up our shaky recollections into an agreement of fact. By the time we reached the truck, we had ourselves a hunting story.

We flopped the deer parts onto the pickup bed and headed for the hot springs a short distance from where we parked. We stripped to skinny dip and clean off the blood from our hands and arms. Our clothes had a funky odor, to be sure. But the geyser's fumes had an overbearing stink. It was called Colter's Hell, part of a geothermal eruption at the mouth of the canyon on the Shoshone River. It had been a popular stopping-off point for mountain men, trappers, and Indian tribes over hundreds of years. Now it was the young white hunters' favorite winter swimming hole. We soaked until close to dusk, then headed back to the truck.

"I'll split the meat with you, Will," said Vincent. Wild game was our social currency and I knew that he was trading for future favors.

"Sounds good. We can hang it in your garage this week and cut it up next weekend," I said.

"Sure. It's going to be cold enough this week, it won't hurt to let the meat age some," he said, "so, let's go out Saturday and bag *your* deer."

BEVERLY: RESCUING THE BOYS

God could not be everywhere, and therefore he made mothers.

— Rudyard Kipling

Will and Vincent had decided to take the old camper trailer of Vincent's dad's out to the area where they hunted deer in the fall. They'd hooked it up to the borrowed pickup that Will's boss used on the ranch, and took off on a Friday night in mid-October, the earliest they could get onto Forest Service land. They said they wanted to get to the Fishhawk Trailhead and set up camp so they could get up early the next morning to hunt. The camping area was about forty-two miles south of Cody, so I felt confident that the old ranch pickup would be reliable enough to get them there and back. I was mistaken. Early Sunday afternoon, the boys straggled into the duplex, worn and haggard.

"What happened," I said making it more of a statement

69

than a question and knowing the answer was not going to be good.

"Truck broke down," the boys said, in unison. "We had to hitchhike out."

"Mom, can you get Leon's truck and help us haul the camper and pickup out of there?" Will's pleading pulled on my heart strings, but all I could think about was that I had to be at work early Monday morning. I couldn't fathom the logistics needed to pull this off on a Sunday night in October when daylight vanished early.

Hoping that the ranch hands were still at the main house having their midday dinner, I called to ask if Leon was there. I heard Alma put the receiver down on the hall table, some footsteps, and muffled voices. Then Leon's voice boomed in my ear.

"Bev, what's the trouble? What did those boys do this time?"

"Nothing they couldn't help, Leon. The old pickup broke down. They had to hitchhike back to town."

"Well, I cain't do anythin' about it," he said in his south Texas drawl. "Ah have to go back to the fields here in a few minutes."

"I know that. I'm just calling to ask if we can borrow your truck to pull the camper out. I don't know what to do about getting that pickup running, though."

"Will better call his boss and see if it's okay to leave the pickup there for a few days. We can get out there this weekend with some tools, try to figure out the problem with it."

"So...can we still come get your truck this afternoon?"

"I guess that's our only option. Just remember to leave your car keys with Alma when you get here so I have a way to drive home tonight."

"Sure, and thanks, Leon." I was grateful that he was still willing to help out with the boys in some ways.

"I'm dropping my keys on Alma's hall table right now," he said and hung up.

After the boys and I barreled out to the ranch to get Leon's truck, we breathed a little easier. But I was still nervous driving that big old Dodge Power Wagon, a manual five-speed. My legs were barely long enough to reach the pedals, and I had to constantly wrestle the gear shifter. The three of us were crammed into the front seat, so every time I shifted gears, I had to shove my shoulder into Vincent's to make room for my elbow and the shifter. The two had "drawn straws" and the loser had to sit in the middle while the winner got the window and more leg room.

"Mom, we're going to have to get you some stilts to reach those pedals," Will teased.

"Believe me, if Leon would have let you drive instead of insisting that I take the wheel, I'd gladly hand it over," I said, feeling my arm getting sore from the push and pull of shifting gears.

"How will he even know if I drove it?" said Will. "Really, Mom. You should let me drive this beast."

"No, I told him I would be the only driver, so that's what we're going to do." I felt like Leon would find out somehow and then there would be hell to pay.

It really wasn't the fact that the pedals were hard to reach, or the gear shifter so stiff that it jarred my arm. The worst part was the play in the enormous steering wheel. I had to constantly move it back and forth just to go straight down the road.

"If you think this is bad," said Vincent, "just wait 'til you start pulling that camper along behind it."

Oh, great, I thought. *Just my luck, I'll put Leon's truck AND the camper in the ditch before this is all over with!*

WILL: GOING TO THE MAT

We're loyal to you, Cody High;
We're gold and blue, Cody High; we'll back you to stand
Against the best in the land
For we know you can stand,
Cody High; Rah, Rah!

— Broncettes' Cheer

The final regular season football game wrapped up in late October, and no sooner had I put the shoulder pads away than I was due to start wrestling practice. There was no break between football season and wrestling season. One ended the week before Halloween, the other started the week after. Both wrestling coaches had their eyes on me, planning my initiation into the heavyweight class.

The first two weeks of practice were the worst ones of

my life. I thought I was in great shape from playing football, but that was nothing compared to the conditioning hoisted upon us by the wrestling coaches. Coach Terry paired each of us underclassmen with the seniors. The triad — Rod, Larry, and Ken — led us around like puppies in the beginning. First, we started off by jogging around the mats in the gym, or if it was nice outside, we ran around the city park. That was followed by "stand up" dynamic stretches, hand fighting drills, and takedowns before hitting the mats for "top and bottom" training.

We'd finally get a short water break; then the coach split us up into groups and gave us different scenarios to practice as if it were a live match. A lot of these scenarios involved getting caught in certain positions and then trying to get out of them. Each practice ended with sprints, suicides, and jump rope.

The whole team started to catch on, and guys in the lower weight classes — 126, 146, 152, and 170 (which was Vincent's) — were expected to be state champs. Week three practices intensified as the coaches picked the varsity squad.

I was going into my junior year of high school. I had grown two inches over the summer and gained forty pounds. There was no doubt in my mind or the coach's that I was taking a varsity position as tackle. Cody High had always done well in football and I wanted to prove myself worthy when I was nominated as all-state tackle. Impressed with that, the two wrestling coaches already had plans for me. I was now a true heavyweight at two hundred and forty pounds. I was happy knowing I didn't have to miss meals and starve myself just to make weight. I got some guff from last year's Junior Varsity heavyweight Dick Ames, who thought he was a shoo-in and expected to take the varsity position. He wasn't counting on the fact he'd have to reckon with me for the spot.

I'd been working on the ranch and throwing hay bales all summer, plus more weekends than I care to count helping Leon to sack sawdust for the oil rigs. I asked him what the roustabouts used them for; he explained that they'd use a concoction of sawdust, water, and concrete to pour down the holes and firm them up. So, Gordy and I would spend all day on the end of a scoop shovel, filling the bags. Once he had a pile of them in the bed of the pickup and on the trailer, Leon would disappear for a few hours to deliver them, and then he'd come back for the next load. We lived like kings off the money he paid us, but Mom also made us save back for things we needed for school.

Leon claimed that shoveling those bags of sawdust would toughen me up, make me a force to be dealt with when I hit the football field and the wrestling mats.

Because of the boxing with Leon, SF#3, all those summer evenings after ranching all day, when he wanted to teach me to fight, to be a tough guy, came in really handy with wrestling. I'd learned to be fast on my feet when sparring with Leon, so I applied some of those same moves to this sport. He'd burned the lessons into my brain.

"Listen to me, bo-ah," his Texas drawl booming at me. "Boxing footwork is all about carrying you in all directions and with timing."

"Yes, sir," I'd say.

"When you use footwork to retreat, remember: You should always do that with the attitude that you are going to advance forward and land your punches."

"Yes, *SIR!*" I always felt like I should be saluting him when he lectured me. Leon definitely had the skill, reflexes, and training to whip my butt.

"You'll see that when you can combine your footwork with timing, you'll control the pace and momentum of the fight." Conserving his energy, he'd circle around me, making sure to stay within range but not compromising his position.

Foolishly, I'd square off and face him straight on, giving him even more angles of attack.

Eventually, though, I learned you shouldn't always be plodding forward just as you shouldn't always be throwing punches. As for timing, you should always use timed footwork. There's no point in just bouncing back and forth wasting energy with no meaning. You should be moving in with a purpose and moving out with a purpose. Simply bouncing around a heavy bag all day doesn't make you a boxer with good footwork.

When I started wrestling, I also saw that intentional moves like parrying came in handy. That's when you deflect your opponent's advance; say he's grabbing for you with his left hand so you use your opposite hand or elbow to direct his grab elsewhere than in your direction. It leaves your opponent unbalanced, giving you more space and time to counter his move as his hands are momentarily out of the way. It's a truly beautiful defensive move.

My teammates teased me about being a twinkle toes, but then they started copying me, trying to imitate my blocks, parries, and feints.

As the third week wrestle-offs started, I intimidated Ames to ensure my position for heavyweight on the varsity squad. Coach Terry was hyped about my potential, and he put in extra time with me, teaching me some moves. Heavyweights don't usually use leg take-downs because it leaves them vulnerable. But I was very quick on my feet and Coach recognized that I had a talent for real footwork.

"Any older and you would have a hard time with the things I'm showing you," Coach told me.

At week four, our Cody team was formed and we wrestled a dual match with the school at Lander, Wyoming. The Junior Varsity matches dragged on, and all of us varsity wrestlers sized up our opponents for later. With four weight classes in the match, Coach concentrated on the other ones; he wasn't focused on my heavyweight match at all. If our Cody team could get two more wins, we'd defeat Lander. While waiting around and chewing the fat with some of the crowd, I found out that their heavy-weight, Nick Walton, was second at State last year and was expected to win it all this year as a senior. I knew I was an unknown, so I readied myself for the final match of the night. We'd already taken the victory, so this match became purely personal.

We stepped onto the mat and I sized him up, shook hands with him, and stepped to the line. Walton strut-ted around for the crowd, and then took the line. The referee whistled the start. Both of us locked arms, testing each other's strength. After several attempts at a throw, Walton broke the hold and when he did, I stepped right and grabbed his leg for a lift and lock at chest high. He was caught off guard and I back-stepped while he fell. Just before he landed, I smashed into his back, pasting him into the mat. He bounced up and I stepped out, throwing my arm under his and over his neck. With a heave and a shot from my chest, Walton rolled to his side. I pushed the half Nelson in deeper to keep his mo-mentum going.

The crowd was aghast at how quickly Walton ended up on his back and on the bottom. I cinched up the half Nelson, went chest to chest with him, legs spread, my full weight pressing his chest. Then I finished him off. I lifted his head and planted my left hand on the mat for balance. Time slowed down. Walton struggled under me, but I pinned him.

My team exploded and the crowd couldn't believe what just happened. As I shook my opponent's hand, I was mobbed by my teammates. Coach stood by, chuckling. He knew what was coming for me.

Two weeks later, Casper had a large multi-team tournament. This would be a real test as the Class A and B and double-A teams met. Nick and I could meet again before the State tournament. Every day was tough, with all-out drills and more drills to build muscle memory and quick reactions. The coaches instructed us on new moves and, more importantly, counter moves. Then, it was drill, drill, drill and physical conditioning.

"This tourney will not set the placing for State, but who's who will be there," Coach told us. "So, wrestling your *best* will make every one of you *better*."

As the date approached, Coach showed me one more move. I took to this one like a duck to water. I was diligent in working to master it. Coach was convinced that my quickness and agility proved me to be an awesome opponent.

Our Cody team signed in at Casper and I found out there were six of us in the heavyweight class. Nick was on the list too. Casper also had a heavyweight—a senior who weighed in at 265 pounds. Every match would count points to the finale. I'd wrestle once on Friday night and two times on Saturday. Championship matches took place on Saturday night.

My Friday night match wasn't easy. We went into three rounds and finished on points. But on Saturday, I made short work of both matches, helping my team get to second place position and only four points behind the leader. With my three wins, I ended up in the heavy class championship match against Casper's 265-pounder.

Before we started, Coach pulled me aside.

"Will, we have five wrestlers in the championship rounds—that's great," said Coach. "But we've fallen back on points, so every one of you boys has to pin your opponent and gain the lead."

As the tournament progressed into evening, two of our Cody wrestlers pinned their man, so at least second place was secured. Then it was time for my match. We started out with a push-and-shove banter with some counterattacks thrown in. Late in the third period, we were tied two-to-two and neither of us giving in. I knew I'd never give up and quit, but on my next move, I slipped and Casper scored two points on me. The tournament ended and we finished in second place overall.

I was hang-dog in the locker room, moping around and cussing under my breath. Coach walked in and pulled me aside.

"Will, remember, second place is good for a first-year varsity wrestler, especially for a tourney of this caliber."

"I know, Coach, and thanks. I just wish I wouldn't have slipped and gave away the points," I mumbled but squared my shoulders up just thinking about Coach's words and his confidence in me.

Back at home, we continued with the same routine—drills and conditioning. Coach started working with me on a number of new moves and pin combinations.

The next week was the Wyoming State Tournament. Early that week, the coach's association compared the eastern and southern divisions, and their votes vaulted our Cody team to first place. But doing this put a target on our backs, so I knew Nick was gunning for me, because he'd worked hard to place for championship status too.

The big day arrived, all the teams converged, and brackets were set. I got a bye for the first round. I was jumpy with waiting around. My Saturday morning match would pit me against a 250-pounder from the southeast division. As it got closer to the start of the match, my nerves got tighter. Vincent saw that I was wound up and tried to calm me down.

Finally, the match began. As we tied up, right away I saw that this joker wasn't very strong and he was chubby to boot. So I ripped a new technique and scored, but no pin. In the second round, I took top and surprised him with a three-quarter Nelson from the side. Then a hip bump rolled him over for my half Nelson and a pin! My second match came up too soon. I was still reminiscing on my last pin when I shook hands with my opponent.

Switch your focus. It's now or never—this match gets you into the championship round.

The whistle sounded and we quickly tied up. Then I beat my opponent by landing a head and arm throw. Coach told me this was a tough move for a heavyweight, but he'd been working with me on hips and throws. Two seconds later, my adversary pounded the mat; I sucked his head and arm up into my chest and leaned back hard. This match was over in very short order.

Cody erupted on the sidelines. *We've taken the lead in points!*

Vincent and I compared our standings. The next match propelled Nick to the championship round too. So, the defining match was set: Nick and I met again, and this time it was for the trophy.

Finally, we faced each other, shook hands, and tied up. Nick pressed for an arm lock and I watched his legs. But I'd worked hard with the coaches on arm locks and I pummeled him out. We got another tie-up, but this time, I snuck in my own head and arm lock, twisting my hips for the throw. Nick countered by dropping his hips and getting a tight waist. Next, I released and twisted back to counter *his* counterattack, but Nick had left his foot solidly planted. Swift as a panther, I snatched his leg and ran the pipe for a single. As Nick hit the mat, I slapped another half Nelson on and pinned him.

Wow! The gym exploded in a frenzy of movement and noise. The match ended, we stood in the center of the mat, and the ref raised my arm high in the air. I nearly fell over with exhilaration—I realized I had just become the new Wyoming Class A heavyweight champion!

Instantly, I scanned the stands for Leon and Mom. *Did they see it? Did they see me?*

I spotted a large, open area in the grandstand. My mom was the sole person standing there cheering with all her might. Coaches were congratulating me and my teammates, and suddenly there was Leon, giving me a bear hug.

"I had to come down here to the floor," he yelled in my ear. "Your mother was beating everyone up there in the bleachers. She cleared out that whole section!"

Tears spilling down my face, I climbed up the bleachers to Mom, giving her a big, sweaty hug. She hugged right back, clinging to my waist, laughing and crying all at the same time.

BEVERLY: MOMS MUST POP ZITS

Good character is not formed in a week or a month. It is created little by little, day by day. Protracted and patient effort is needed…

— Heraclitus

I'm watching Will as he walks onto the wrestling mat to face his challenger—this is the deciding match. Beads of sweat gather on my forehead and I'm sure he's feeling the same. Will he be the next State Champion? My heart balloons with pride as I watch him. What started a decade ago with him wrestling his little brother to the floor at home has culminated in this moment that I pray will be his glory.

When my son was little I could wrap my arms around him several times a day and he willingly accepted my outward affection. Now that he's become a teenager, the manner in which he shows affection toward me and also the way he allows me to show affection toward him has changed dramatically.

Every once in a while, I'm fortunate enough to receive a warm hug, which always puts a smile on my face. His bulky arms wrap around me somewhat awkwardly with his face turned slightly away as if to say, "Sorry, Mom... that's all I've got for you today."

When it comes to teen boys, "hugs" — albeit, not the traditional kind — come in all shapes and sizes.

Sometimes it comes in the form of a limp pat on the back as I wrap my arms around him. Other times, it's when he asks for a back rub after a long day or maybe it's a gentle elbow nudge when you're both laughing at a joke.

I have found that no matter how old my son gets, he still needs my touch, which doesn't mirror today what it did when he was a toddler or even when he was in elementary school. In fact, it has changed immensely just over the past couple of years. But I've come to realize that even though he's growing up and on the cusp of becoming a man, he still needs the feel of my physical contact with him.

Lately, some of our closest moments have been when I sit him down to cut his hair.

Will is very particular about this. Even though his wrestling coach wants all of the boys to have short crew cuts, Will insists on a sleek, side part with tapered back and sides.

"Mom! Don't shave it like I'm going to boot camp!

The flat-top look just isn't cool. I still want some hair left on my head," he groans as I whisk the plastic cape around him and (barely) snap it shut at his neck. I ignore the comment.

"I'm going to have to move the snap on this cape," I say. "Your neck is growing as fast as the rest of you!"

"Well, I *am* the only heavyweight wrestler on the team," he gloats. "It seems logical that my neck muscles would grow along with the rest of me."

As all of my boys crept through elementary and into middle and high school, I noticed a definite shift in the appearance department. Will was the most particular of the three—neither Dean nor Gordy took such an in-depth interest in their hair and hygiene. When he was in junior high and didn't yet have his driver's license, my middle son once had me pull my car over. He unbuckled his seat belt and checked his hair in the rearview mirror before he got out of the car at the school yard. Even today his bathroom looks like a beauty salon with the assortment of hair products, powders, deodorant, anti-itch cream, and who knows what else.

That doesn't come close to his body odor obsession. One minute, I've got this dirty child who hasn't washed his body orifices thoroughly for thirteen years, and then suddenly, he discovers the manly thrill of deodorant. Now, at sixteen, he's even more obsessive.

As I take the clippers and the electric trimmer to his hair, Will comments about some of the smellier classmates he contends with in school.

"We call Darrell Robinson 'Ramsbottom' because he smells like a goat's butt." Will snickers, a bit embarrassed that he's ratting out Darrell to me. "His mom won't let him wear deodorant."

"What happens to boys who smell bad?" I ask.

"We call him 'Schwet-i-ie,'" he says, holding his nose, "and pass someone's deodorant over to him." He states this in a matter-of-fact way, implying that I'm not keeping up with the times.

He won't admit it, but Will is worried about his own under-body odors. I know he uses enormous amounts of Dr. Scholl's odor-eaters underfoot, deodorant underarm, and Gold Bond under testicles.

Vitalis for hair styling and Aqua Velva for a bracing aftershave are standard fare, too. The bottles line up on the shelf above the bathroom sink. We have only one bathroom to share amongst us, so there are no secrets when it comes to who's using which personal freshness products.

Then comes the moment.

"Mom, can you check my back and see if there are blackheads?"

I know all about his fruitless daily routine with the endless assaults on blackheads which, like hydras, seemed to spring up tenfold for every one squeezed. His obsession with his acne-stricken features doesn't surprise me. I've already been through this routine with his older brother Dean.

His tactic, to offset the zit attack, is to shower multiple times each day. I know, from previous experience with said older brother Dean, that it is wholly natural for the male adolescent to be obsessed with showering. Will's frequency of showers has increased exponentially with his age. My guess is that now that he is sixteen, he's lying to his friends to show that he doesn't care about personal cleanliness.

But at this state, he's doing anything in his power to offset the hideous effects of full-blown puberty. His sweat glands start going into overdrive, causing his armpits and feet and crotch to reek and his once-smooth prepubescent features to resemble something like the aftermath of the campaign of the First World War, fraught with pockmarks and noticeable indentations.

I know from many nights of cape-wrapping haircuts with Will that he thinks about this dilemma constantly. He is definitely worried about whether his "spots" are showing. He would not, however, talk about it with any of his buddies at school.

Secretly, Will indulges in what he deems girlie rituals: He collects an array of moisturizers, scrubs, and face packs as he tries to eradicate his own experience with zit hell. I've noticed, though, that much like chemical fertilizers, the more he uses those popular products, the more he *has* to use them. First, he uses some type of alcohol-based cleanser that makes his face crusty. Then, he uses moisturizer to counteract the effects of the cleanser. He's pleased with how his skin looks at first, but ultimately, his face erupts once again into horrid, subcutaneous pustules. My cure: plain old soap and water. *But will he listen to me, his mother?* No, of course not!

I don't have the nerve to tell him that he's guaranteed to get spots whatever he does, so he may as well grin and bear it. But nearly every morning I catch him attacking the little black wrigglers that congregate around his nose, or those puffy ones on his chin that explode onto the mirror.

That's when I think: *Raising boys involves a lot of revolting things when you're the mom.* I end up being the one to grin and bear it, not him. It doesn't make me love him less. In fact, I am enamored with the miracle in my life that I call "my son."

WILL: KINGS AND COWBOYS

*"You're good, kid, but as long as I'm around, you're second-best.
So you may as well learn to live with it."*

— the Man in The Cincinnati Kid

Hunting season ended, the holidays were behind us, and wrestling was over for the year. Boredom set in on a late winter's Friday night with nothing to do. All four of us ended up at Floyd's house and decided on five-card draw, Joker's wild.

We piled downstairs into Floyd's basement—aptly named Floyd's Hole—where he had the perfect set-up for poker: a felt-covered tabletop, a mini-fridge stocked with soda pops (and cans of Schlitz hidden behind them), plus enormous bags of potato chips.

Before we settled in at the poker table, we slung some zingers back and forth.

I popped open my first beer and guzzled half of it so

I could let loose my virgin burp of the evening—a long, loud "B-bb—rr—ra—a—acckk" right into Baxter's face.

He retorted by swinging his butt around, hitting the fridge door so it shut, and putting me directly downwind of his horrendous fart. It was amazing how fast he could stink up a room.

"Jesus H. Christ, Baxter!" I covered my face with my T-shirt. "What crawled up your butt and died?"

We all scrambled over to the window, and Vincent cranked it open as we gasped for fresh air.

"Nothin' died, you moron. I just ate the school lunch today—chili and cinnamon rolls—yum!" Baxter strutted slowly away from the fridge, apparently oblivious to the stench that trailed after him.

I could tell this night was going to be a beer-fueled expedition into toilet humor. There would be no meaningful conversation about feelings, dreams, or relationships. There would, however, be plenty of talk about farting, snot, and making out with girls.

We figured out what the table stakes were, and then Baxter dealt first. Not only did we have our stacks of poker chips in front of us, but also an array of potato chip crumbs, which Floyd had spewed across the table as he gorged. He hadn't even taken one breath since he started shoving them into his mouth.

"Holy crap, Floyd! I'm going to call you Alvin the Chipmunk from now on," Vincent said as he swiped the spittle-encrusted bits off the table.

Floyd's stuffed cheeks didn't stop him from cussing at Vincent and telling him to shut his trap.

After four or five hands, Vincent sat with a short stack in front of him, outflanked and battling our smart-ass comments. His fuse burned to a stub the more we ribbed him.

"What's wrong, little girl?" Floyd looked at Vincent with a long face. "Cards not cooperating for you?"

"Shut up, you wart-hog," Vincent said, his eyes dark as he glared at the hand he was dealt. "Dammit! I'm down two racks and I ain't won a pot yet."

"Give them a really good scramble this time, Will," Baxter said. "No, I mean really shuffle those cards!" Baxter had been holding his own ground until now, but he knew where the showdown was shaping up. Floyd and I exchanged a glance: Amateurs like Baxter are easy to exploit. We knew we could take advantage of his whining to spur him into making dumb mistakes.

I don't want to berate my pal for playing badly, but let's face it, the skill needed for winning at poker is not only mathematical mastery but also tempting the other guy to make a different decision than he normally would while he's under pressure of losing all his chips. With an unspoken agreement, Floyd and I ganged up on Baxter.

"Unless you're holding at least six tits in your hand," said Floyd, looking at Baxter, "you might want to just fold this time."

"He's bluffing, buddy," I said. "He doesn't have three

queens, no way!"

To be sure, luck is also a fact of poker: it's like gravity — it's there and you have to deal with it and you have to work within its realities.

Before I could shuffle the cards for the next hand, the basement door creaked open. We rushed to hide our beers and set our soda pop cans on the table.

Floyd's mom hailed from the top of the stairs, "Hi, boys, I just need to get some clothes out of Floyd's hamper to fill up the washer." She clumped down the steps and peered at us as she was passing through to get to the bedroom.

"You boys aren't getting into mischief down here, are you?" She smiled at us. This was her standard statement, but we all knew she was spying on us and trying to detect whether we'd been into the "hidden" beer.

"No, of course not, Mrs. Jenson," we answered in unison.

She disappeared into Floyd's room for a quick minute; then came out clinging to a bundle of jockey shorts, T-shirts, jeans, and socks.

Floyd jumped up and ran over to her, setting off a tug of war.

"Geez, Mom!" He glared at her as he tried to grab a piece of cloth from her hands. "This shirt's still fine to wear — it's just a little wrinkled."

Floyd's mom studied the shirt, but held on tight. "Floyd. Honey. That shirt's been laying on the floor all week and now it's wrinkled beyond the salvage stage. I'm not going to try to save it by ironing it."

"Mom," he groaned. "Just leave the jeans then."

"No!" She pulled harder on the leg of the jeans, and they grappled for a stronger hold. Floyd's pants were now doing the splits. "They have a big ketchup stain! I'll have to oxidize them."

Floyd loosened his grasp reluctantly, and his mom clutched them close to her chest. He eyed the other gobs of material that she'd seized from his hamper.

"Don't even try to convince me that you can re-wear these jockey shorts. The funk seeping out of them could gag a gorilla."

We appreciated Mrs. Jenson's humor and by now we were cat-calling at Floyd and mimicking him.

"Aw, c'mon, Mom! Pleeezzz let me wear my stinky shorts one more day!" Vincent howled at the ceiling.

Baxter and I sniggered at Vincent's impersonation.

During the fray, she'd dropped some items on the floor and was now scooping them up and stuffing them into the bundle. "And I just can't believe how many socks that dryer eats," she said on her way to the stairs. "Every time I wash, there's at least a half-dozen mismatched pairs."

This last comment triggered a roar of laughter from us. We knew the truth. *Floyd* was the missing sock thief, not the dryer. We knew exactly what happened to those socks. Baxter's hand started pumping up and down, the universal sign we all knew. Another burst of laughter exploded.

We finally got ourselves put back together enough to play cards again. Everybody anted up and Vincent dealt five cards facedown for each player. Baxter sat to Vincent's left, so he got to bet first. Instead, he checked and stayed in the hand for free. I got three tens and a couple of mismatched low cards. I bet anyway, hoping for four of a kind in the draw to replace my two duds. Floyd and Vincent matched my bet and we started the draw round. Baxter went first again. He threw in four cards and Vincent dealt the replacements. I tossed in two cards and Vincent shot two my way. Then Floyd threw in one card and the new one slid across the felt, where he stacked it on top of the other four without looking at it. Vincent stood pat, a surprise to all of us.

We started the second and final betting round. Baxter folded, shaking his head and grumbling about his luck. I bet again. Floyd pulled his last card slowly toward his others, peeked at the top of the card, and let out a big, noisy sigh like he missed the draw. But he stayed in and bet too. Vincent matched the bet, so the three of us went to the showdown.

Floyd threw his last card over, followed by his others, showing two pair—kings and jacks. Smirking, he started raking in the chips.

"Wait just a minute, asshole!" I yelled, turning my cards up. "Three of a kind trumps your kings and cowboys!"

Vincent couldn't compete with either of us, so he

folded at this point. But nobody was paying attention to him because Floyd and I were hollering at each other.

Confusion ensued, and we all talked at once. Baxter was in Floyd's camp and Vincent took up my side of the argument.

"Kings and cowboys lose!" Vincent slammed his hands onto the table. The chips chattered and danced and we fell silent.

"The hell it does!" Floyd snarled back, cheeks puffing and red-faced.

"Okay, okay, let's settle this the right way," said Baxter. "I'll call my uncle Vic. He lived in Vegas and played the tables a lot."

Baxter thumped up the stairs to use the phone in the kitchen. We trailed after him so we could all hear what his uncle told him.

"You got any milk and Hershey's syrup here?" I asked Floyd. I'd overdosed on beer and chips, and now I needed something to coat my belly.

"Sure," he said. We were in an argument, but still friendly. "The chocolate syrup is in that cabinet up on the right." There was no hint of malice in his voice.

While I took a swig from the milk carton to test its freshness, Vincent was parked in front of the hallway mirror and had commenced popping a few ripe zits and auguring his left ear to clear some waxy buildup.

I set the milk down and pounced on him, aiming my punch for his crotch. He ducked away at the last second, so I tackled him and reached around the floor for a make-shift weapon with which to castrate him. This was our usual tussle, and, as teenage boys, we were obsessed with violence and erogenous zones, though we were careful not to place a faggot hold on the other guy. All of these antics were meant to avoid any sharing of inner-most thoughts and fears with each other. To do so was a sign of weakness, and the offender would be summarily maligned.

"Uncle Vic!" Baxter boomed into the orange wall phone. "My buddies and I are playing five-card draw, Joker's wild, and we have a question about a hand."

Vincent and I broke apart and we all huddled around the earpiece to hear what his uncle had to say.

Baxter explained and then asked, "So, does Floyd deserve to win that hand?"

Uncle Vic's voice buzzed through from the other end. "Nope. Even though Floyd has two pair, even if they are kings and cowboys, the three of a kind trumps them."

"You've gotta be shittin' me," groaned Floyd, turning away from the phone and glowering at me.

"My thirty miles of bad road wins!" I bulldozed toward Floyd, hoping to knock him off balance, but he sidestepped and I slammed into the wall. Floyd's school photo shook and tilted from the vibration. The guys were splitting a gut over this, so I coolly straightened the frame and we thundered back down the stairs to finish the game.

BEVERLY: MY SON HAS
A CRUSH ON A GIRL

*It is an extra dividend when you like
the girl you've fallen in love with.*

— Clark Gable

Will's first girlfriend, at least the first one I knew about, was Teddie Joy. I didn't see her much outside of the after-school activities, the ball games, or the wrestling matches. At first, I liked her a lot. She was a smart girl and when I heard my son talking to her on the phone every night, he seemed happy. After a while, Teddie Joy started calling our house nearly a dozen times a night. I thought: Oh, that's cute! She's so smitten with Will! Then the calls became intrusive. Teddie Joy would yell at whoever answered the phone if we didn't disclose Will's whereabouts immediately. Then I noticed Will apologizing a lot when he talked to Teddie Joy on the phone.

"Will, why are you always telling Teddie Joy you're sorry?" I asked. "What's going on?"

"Mom, I really don't know. She's always mad at me and I don't know why."

Now I was worried. I didn't want to forbid him from seeing her, because that may make her even more attractive to him. But I also didn't want to say nothing, because this is not the way relationships are built. It helped that Gordy kept telling Will that she was mean and even a little scary. At least I wasn't the only one who thought so!

The final straw broke when I went over to the school one day to watch Will and the other boys at football practice. When it was over, I watched as Will walked over to Teddie Joy. She was scowling, standing with her back to him. He said something to her, and she didn't acknowledge him, so he walked away, head bent down.

Later that night at home, I asked him what that was all about.

"Oh, nothing. She's just mad at me again."

"Why? Did you two have an argument or something?"

"No. I was supposed to meet her after school by the back door, but I was late."

"Oh?" I didn't want to pry too much, but I wanted him to keep talking.

"I had to stay after and talk to one of my teachers. It only took five minutes, but now she won't even talk to me."

"What do you think you should do?" I asked.

"I don't know," he said and hung his head. "I can't do anything right by her."

Gordy, who'd been absorbing our conversation, piped in. "You have to dump that girl!" he exclaimed.

Will sighed and shuffled off to his room.

The phone rang and I could almost detect that it was Teddie Joy on the other end of the line. I picked up the receiver, and before I could get it to my ear, she screamed at me to put Will on the phone.

"Teddie Joy. I don't accept this kind of thing from my own children and I won't accept it from you, either." I hung up. The phone rang a half-dozen times, then went silent.

Will mustered the courage to call her back later that night. He "broke up" with her—basically, I heard him tell her she wasn't nice and that he really didn't like her anymore. Teddie Joy hasn't called our house since then.

Will took to spending time with his other male friends, and the winter was quiet when it came to the girls.

Later in the spring, after wrestling was finished, he started seeing Christine. I was relieved. She was really a nice girl and her father was the sheriff. I knew then that Will couldn't get into any pickles with this girlfriend.

WILL: DREAM GIRL

Age does not protect you from love.
But love, to some extent, protects you from age.

— Jeanne Moreau

Winter morphed into spring. It was a warm May evening and I decided to walk to Christine's house. Her dad had already agreed to loan us his car for our Saturday night date. I spotted her as soon as I turned in to the driveway—absolutely gleaming, the late afternoon sun reflecting off her features. There she was, my dream girl—pure and neat as a new pin—yet luring me with the curve of her lines. She was a sleek but surprisingly powerful thing, with style and a flair for velocity. She was a sexy package, all right, and the thrill of being near her electrified me.

The screen door squeaked open. I tore my eyes away from the object of my desire. Christine burst down the steps and planted herself in front of me, blocking my view of her dad's patrol car.

"Flirting with the Fire Puff again, are you?" She swaggered to the car, sweeping her hand along the front panel and leaning over to caress the hood. "I'm not sure if you really like *me,* or just my wheels!"

"Oh, come on, Christine. You know I love you both."

She giggled and stuck out her tongue. "You big goon, let's get going. It's almost time for the movie to start."

I dug the fact that I was dating one of the most popular girls in school, Christine Kingsley. She was a fox, but sort of a dangerous one — her father was a cop. You really had to watch your P's and Q's around him. Sheriff Kingsley was suspicious about everything and asked a ton of questions every time I came by to pick Christine up for our dates. He had the same tough stare that Bullitt — you know, Steve McQueen — had in his cop movies. He was constantly scanning for nefarious activity while standing on the front porch with me. He never let his guard down, and he was rock solid. He'd pound his fist on his chest and tell me, "Every cop has to stay in shape so he can chase down the dirtbags on foot if he has to." After he was around me for a while, though, he seemed to relax his military "commander" approach and we'd shoot the breeze.

After moving his wife and daughter to our town five years earlier, Kingsley discovered that the Sherriff's Department in Cody couldn't afford to supply the men with police cruisers, so he'd had to buy one of his own. He was as protective of his patrol car as he was his daughter, but eventually he trusted me enough to loan his squad car to Christine and me for special dates, like tonight.

It was cool to cruise around in the Fire Puff, but it had its drawbacks too. I couldn't burn rubber. When guys like Floyd Jenson pulled up at the stoplight beside us, revving the engine on his '62 Chevy Impala and taunting me, all I could do was wave and flip him the bird. It wasn't like the squad car didn't have the power to pound Floyd's Chevy into the pavement—Christine's dad had acquired a powerful 1960 Plymouth Pursuit Special Golden Commando 395. Those were usually reserved for patrols on superhighways. How he ever ended up with that car in the middle of Wyoming is a mystery to me. But it sure was cool when Christine and I ran it out to Buffalo Bill Dam in the wee hours of the morning.

Usually, when Christine's dad *did* decide to toss the keys over to me, he'd have a story to tell before letting us walk out the door. Tonight had been no exception. I didn't mind hanging around for a few minutes, but Christine was antsy. She kept running upstairs to check her makeup or grab her sweater, or whatever else girls do in anticipation of a make-out session.

Christine's dad and I ambled out to the porch; I leaned against the post while he settled into the swing, puffing on a cig.

"I was a Nevada State Trooper in '57. We lived up on

the northeast shore of Lake Tahoe, in a little town by the name of Incline Village. I patrolled Mount Rose Highway twice a day. It's just a two-laner with a lot of snaky bends. It takes you over the highest mountain pass in the Sierra Nevada and connects with Reno on the other side. From the summit — it's about 8,900 feet — there's a twenty-five-mile stretch of road on a steep grade. At the bottom you end up at a suburb of Reno called Galena.

"Early one morning in June, I met a tractor-trailer coming down the mountain. The driver was waving wildly at me. I knew his brakes had gone out, so I wheeled around in a bootlegger's turn at forty miles an hour and punched it. I pushed my brand-new Dodge D-500 to try to catch the runaway truck. The pointer hovered at ninety, the maximum on the speedometer. Then I got blocked by oncoming traffic, so I had to stay in line behind the eighteen-wheeled monster for about five miles. I clocked it at eighty miles per hour, and it was speeding up."

"Man, that sounds crazy. What did you do?" I asked.

"I figured out a plan while I followed him. I knew that my patrol car was the high-performance model — it had really stiff front coil springs and heavy-duty shock absorbers front and rear. The stabilizer bar was sturdy and added some heft to the frame. But most important, it also had the upgraded brakes: Chrysler twelve-inch drums that were made special for Dodge police cars.

"As soon as I could, I accelerated past and got in front of him. Sixty tons of rolling menace roared behind me. I backed off the throttle real slow and let the tractor's front bumper contact the rear of my squad car. I started pumping the brake pedal, keeping the front bumper of the truck against my car. At first, it didn't seem to do anything. Smoke was coming from all four tires, but we did start to slow down. I watched my speedometer: eighty... seventy-five...sixty... and finally down to thirty miles an hour. Then the driver downshifted his transmission and used the soft edge of the road to stop."

"Wow! You must have been ready to piss your pants!" I was impressed — Christine's dad had balls — you had to give him that.

"It was a good thing I got him stopped when I did, because the Dodge had precious little left to give. Right after that, the two front tires blew out from the terrific heat. The fins and trunk were smashed in, but those brakes saved our lives! If that road rocket had run through Galena, who knows how many could have been hurt or killed? Bashed, bruised, and burnt out as she was, after the tires were changed and some body work, the mechanics brought her back to the station good as new."

"I can't believe you had the nerve to do that — sounds more like a death wish to me!" *This was going to make a good one to tell the guys later.*

"You just do what you have to do — you don't really think about it at the time. You kids take care, now. I don't want to hear about any shenanigans with my daughter *or* my Fire Puff!"

"You've got my word, Mr. Kingsley. I'll bring them both home safe and sound."

We hopped into the squad car and turned the radio up to "our song." It summed up the truth about how I felt about Christine: I might not remember when Columbus sailed the ocean or how to pronounce *"je ne sais quoi"* but I *did* know what was really important — my love for Christine. That night I was going to ask her to go steady. We'd been building up to this since I became a regular fixture on her front porch. We'd snuggle in the swing, sneaking a few wary kisses until her dad would erupt through the front screen door. He'd join us for chitchat and a quick smoke. Then, with a serious glare my way, he'd announce that the new episode of *The Fugitive* was starting on TV. We'd groan in unison and shuffle into the house.

My mind wandered back to last week's show. It was really choice, and secretly, I was glad I hadn't missed it: *Kimball is closing in on the one-armed man, asking about his prey at a diner when a stove catches fire. Kimball runs to help the cook and the stove blows up in his face. In the hospital, Kimball is treated like a ping-pong ball: there's a heated argument between a sympathetic social worker and an icy psychiatrist using Kimball as a case to build his reputation. The accident sets him back and the one-armed man gets away again.* (Which was good, because there would be another episode next week.)

We cruised along Main Street to kill time until the

movie started, when we spotted a group of our school chums. We stopped in the parking lot and the Clark girl waved at me. Christine flashed daggers at me.

"Wanda and I are just lab partners." I looked Christine in the eye. "Nothing else."

"She sure looks like she's got a thing for you," Christine huffed, craning her neck to see if Wanda was still watching us drive away.

I didn't want anything or anyone to get in the way of me getting close to Christine. I'd had a hankering for her ever since I laid eyes on her in junior high, and now that I had her attention, I wasn't letting go. Going steady appealed a lot to me. It was such a drag to compete with the other guys to get a date, especially the proms and formal dances. If Christine was my girl, I wouldn't have to worry about that anymore.

I just couldn't figure out how I was going to pop the question. And when I did, would she say yes?

We parked the Fire Puff, bought our tickets and treats, found our favorite dark corner, and now sat entwined as much as we could over the stiff metal arms of theater chairs.

I leaned in toward Christine, going for our first kiss, when a preview of *The Unsinkable Molly Brown* started up. Christine's head swerved to the screen. In between giggles, she compared her best friend to Molly Brown.

"You should see how she tries to schmooze Mrs. North…"

Watching Christine's mouth move while she talked, I tuned out and didn't hear another thing she said. I just kept thinking, *I can't wait to kiss her!* I'd tried to manufacture a kiss somewhere between the trading of tickets and treats, but it didn't work out. Now, I made a pledge with myself: *You must kiss her in the next minute.* Luckily, the movie started and Christine unsuspectingly threw me a bone.

When the slimy, hollow-eyed sea monster popped onto the screen, she clutched my arm and buried her face in my shoulder. I cupped my hand and, with a gentle nudge, brought her chin up and made serious eye contact with her. I bent forward; her eyes dropped and my lips brushed against hers. I deepened the pressure and she returned it. Before long, we were lip-locked. I wanted to make sure that she forgot about everything else but me.

When Christine and I walked out of the movie, the town was hopping. Before we could get through the parking lot to her dad's patrol car, Carl Tucker pulled up in his orange-flamed '55 Lancer wagon and waved us over.

"Hey, did you hear that Eddie Cochrane is going to challenge Juan Sanchez? They're supposed to drag race at North 18th Road at ten o'clock sharp—and they're racing for *pinks*! The winner gets the other guy's *car*!" Carl tried burning rubber, but the station wagon coughed and sputtered out of the parking lot, the hubcap flippers waving like tiny pinwheels. We could barely see the flamboyant paint job through the trail of smoke from the tailpipe.

"Why in the world does he think that crop duster is a first-rate coupe?" Christine shook her head as she slipped into the seat beside me.

"I have no idea. He spent all that money on pretty chrome goodies, but it's all show and no go with Carl. That car is so lame it wouldn't get out of its *own* way."

We headed down Main Street to check out the rest of the crowd. Word was already all over town. A few of the guys were shooting the breeze in front of the Geyser Drive-In. We coasted past and heard them boasting about how Eddie was going to blow the doors off the bean wagon in the drag race.

The Sanchez kid was sort of a friend of mine—we sparred with the gloves on once in a while, down at the gym, and he was a fair fighter. His Corvair 500 Deluxe was channeled, lowered all the way around like all the other Hispanic dragsters, but his was the newer, sportier Monza. He claimed it was the first production car with turbo, fully independent suspension on each wheel, and four on the floor. All I knew was that it was fast off the line.

I had to admit, though, that my money was on Eddie. His '55 Chrysler C-300 with its Hemi-head V-8 made his ride the winner in my book. I just happened to stop by the shop earlier in the week when Eddie was changing the exhaust system. He'd put cutouts in front of the muffler that opened the exhaust pipe to let the engine breathe easier. It added horsepower and a whole lot of noise. He'd also mounted a blower between the intake manifold and the injectors that pumped more air into the engine and boosted the power from the gas without letting it flood. I knew it was the fastest rod on the street these days.

It wasn't even going to be a close race — Eddie was going to cream Sanchez. *This was going to be fun.*

"Crap!" I'd forgotten we had the squad car for the evening. "How're we going to get out there to the drag without everybody giving us shit for showing up in the black-and-white?"

"Well, how about if we just volunteer to block the road at the finish line and run the cherry light and siren just for fun?" Christine always came up with the greatest ideas.

On the way out of town, we got stuck behind a Chinese Fire Drill. Sue Burton had a carload of girls stuffed into her mom's Renault. At the stoplight, everyone on the driver's side got out and ran around to the passenger's side. Everyone on the passenger's side got out and ran to the driver's side. It reminded me of musical chairs in grade school. We split a gut laughing when Bertha "Sweat Hog" Harriman almost didn't squeeze back in, but she finally oozed into the backseat.

We tooled down to the far end of Main Street and saw Peterson in his pony car, a Mustang 428 Super Cobra Jet, and his rival Bob "Brody" Wyatt facing off in a round of chicken. We pulled over to watch. Brody was in his '64 Olds Starfire Coup.

"I stopped at his house the other day when he was working on it. I'm telling you, Christine, that V8 has a powerful 394 engine, a center console with tachometer, and a floor shifter for the Hydramatic transmission. He can do zero to sixty in nine seconds flat!"

They were both booking straight for each other and it looked like neither was going to give. At the last second, Brody pulled to the side, but not far enough. His mirror exploded, splinters sparkling in my headlights like snowflakes.

"Wow!" exclaimed Christine. "If this is the way the night's starting *out*, I can't wait to see what happens with Juan and Eddie!" We were both eager and ready for the "show after the show."

Road 18 was straight and flat, perfect for drag racing. A ten o'clock race time meant the road had to be lined with cars with their headlights on to light up the track. A rowdy bunch of onlookers had already showed up and were jostling for position along the road. We turned on the siren and plowed through the crowd to the finish line. I saluted the girls and flipped the bird to the guys, glorying in the fact that every man was jealous of my ride *and* my date.

I ran the patrol car well past the quarter-mile marker down the road before pulling it across the lanes to block traffic. It was unlikely anyone would come along; there was only one old retired couple who lived in a small house where the pavement ended.

When Christine and I got back to the starting line, Sanchez and Cochrane were already going at it.

"Hey, *Coch-man*, you dumb candy-ass," Sanchez sneered at Eddie over the roof of his dragster. "You may as well take that junker to the bone yard right now and forget about racing tonight." Sanchez's barrio buddies cheered and joined in with their own slurs: "*Hey, Pachuco!*" and "*Majadero.*"

"By the time you get that lead sled of yours in gear, I'll be crossing the finish line, dip stick." Eddie didn't have the command of cool-talk like Sanchez did, but he still got his digs in. A roar went up from the crowd of Eddie admirers.

Just then, Julie "JJ" Johnson made her entrance onto the blacktop, ready to signal the start of the showdown. In full regalia, her tanned skin glowed against the white leather miniskirt and bolo jacket. Her waist-length platinum mane fluttered in the night breeze. White go-go boots brought her to a full six foot six, taller than most of the school's basketball players. Nobody noticed the flags in her hands. All eyes — at least all *male* eyes — were only on the palomino, drooling over every foot stomp and hand wave as she tried to quiet the crowd.

Headlights flashed and horns blasted down the line, a giant wave of light and noise, signaling that everybody was ready to witness the battle. Arms raised, flags crossed above her head, JJ readied the racers for the countdown. Engines revved, Cochrane and Sanchez inched to the line, glaring sideways at each other, ignoring the roar from the crowd. A half mile away, the squad car's cherry blinked red. In less than thirty seconds, the winner would cross the line. Exhaust ballooned behind the racers; JJ swept the flags in an arc to her knees; tires shrieked against blacktop. Cochrane fishtailed the Chrysler, almost ramming Juan's rear panel, but straightened it out and blew ahead of the Monza. Sanchez slapped the pedal into the floorboard, gaining twenty yards, but still a car length behind Eddie. Ten seconds to the line, a tire exploded, and the Chrysler ground into the pavement, jerking to the left and threatening to roll. Pure adrenaline and instinct took over—Eddie manhandled the steering wheel, cranking it to the right and forcing the car into a lopsided limp to the finish line. Sanchez sailed across the line five feet in front of the Chrysler's grill.

Simultaneous moans and cheers rose into the night sky. Sanchez supporters whooped and threw baseball caps toward the stars, dancing around their cars and kissing girls. Eddie's friends kicked toes in the dirt, mumbling, "Tough break," "He had him hands down," and already campaigning for a re-match. Cochrane, however, leaped out of his injured racecar and bounded across the center line, reaching through the Corvair's window to shake Sanchez's hand.

"You won fair and square, man. Sorry to have to hand her over with her broken leg."

"No, I couldn't take her this way," said Sanchez. "That was some choice driving — you kept your cool. We could've both been blown off the road tonight. Thanks, Cochrane."

Christine ran over to them, hopping up and down, grabbing Eddie's arm. The crowd swarmed around both cars then and Christine evaporated from my sight. Excited as I was to witness Eddie's expert maneuvers and his style in conceding the race to Juan, something didn't feel right; it was like I was out of sync with everything around me. I stopped and turned away from the crowd, looking up into the night sky. The noise from the commotion dimmed.

I was back at the 7D Ranch the summer I worked out there for old man Larson. I'd just finished the upper meadow and had pulled the rake tines up. I noticed the gas cap was loose, so I stood up and reached over to grab it. I lost my footing — it was slick as snot — and slipped under the damned tractor. When I went down, the back tire lumped straight across my chest. Larson was just coming out to pick me up, saw the whole thing, and hauled me into town. My mom and little sister drove up about the same time we pulled under the canopy at the emergency room. My pasty face must have really scared my little sis. I heard her exclaim to Mom, "He looks dead!" but I gimped out of the hospital that day with only a sprained ankle and tractor tire ruts across my chest.

A hand grabbed my arm from behind, jolting me from my reverie. It was Christine.

"Come on, Will. Let's get out of here," she said, shivering as she stared at me. "Are you all right? You seem sort of out of it."

"Yeah, sure, I'm okay. I was just thinking about the time out at old Larson's place when I fell off the tractor and sprained my ankle. I don't know what made me think of that."

"Well, I'm ready to cuddle up on the front seat of the Fire Puff while you drive me home," she said, pulling on my arm.

I had planned this night as the one to ask her to go steady with me, but something held me back. I chickened out and just wrapped my arm around her as she scooted over on the front seat toward me.

We turned the radio on to the tragic and popular song about two teens who crashed their car as the boy swerved to miss another car stalled in the road; the boy crawls over and holds his girl as she dies in his arms.

It was a somber ride home after that.

WILL: THE GAMBLERS

Nobody is always a winner, and anybody who says he is,
is either a liar or doesn't play poker.

— Amarillo Slim

Forty minutes and fifty miles earlier, Vincent and I had ducked out of the Cody High track meet, scored some beer from the local bum looking to make a buck, and were on our way to Red Lodge. Eddie had been helping me tune up my "Baby Cadillac"—a cherry red '57 Chevy Sport Sedan. He showed me how to adjust the fuel injection level on the engine—a Blue Flame Six. Not only did it run smoother than a V-8, but with the four-speed manual transmission and 270 horses with limited slip differential, it had amazing power on the drag strip. I wanted to take her out for a spin, and Vincent was on the hunt for girls. I wasn't really into picking up girls since I started dating Christine, but thought it might help my best friend out if he could score with a nice chick (which didn't happen often for Vincent). As we slugged down our first can of Blue Ribbon, he begged me again to tell him my divorcée story.

"Geez, Vincent, you've heard it a thousand times," I stalled. "It's old news." Flashes of my secret encounters with Mrs. Emerson cropped up in my mind. The first time she called Principal Fish, his office aid Tammy Stewart told me later that she listened in on the secretary's phone. She said that Mrs. Emerson told Fish, "Boys need an education. But they also need a sense of responsibility — a job — something to answer for. I'm a widow with no man in the house. Will can take on some of these duties and help me." Every Thursday, I had an early out from study hall. Every Thursday at 2 p.m. she would call the school, and with her honey-sweet voice, she'd persuade the principal to relinquish me to her.

"Okay, sure," said Vincent. "I get why you were excused from school. Now, get to the good stuff!" You had to hand it to Vincent. He was persistent.

I'd go to her house, walk up on the front porch, and ring the doorbell. Usually, at that time of day, nobody was around, but I'd get the heebie-jeebies just thinking about Fish or one of the teachers spotting me. I'd fidget on the stoop waiting for her to come to the door. As she pushed open the screen door, tilting her head back, she'd gaze at me, her eyes half closed.

"Will. How nice that you could come by and help me today."

Her scent mesmerized me, and all my senses went into overdrive. *Baby, I Need Your Lovin' — Got to Have All Your Lovin'* —I distinctly heard all four Temptations crooning in the dark behind her and swallowing every ounce of fortitude as I stood at the door.

"Yeah, but it's so cool that you had sex when you were just—what—fifteen?" Vincent's voice jerked me back to present. "What I wouldn't give to have an older woman show me the ropes!"

"Well, yeah, I guess so."

"So, what did you do? Did she *really* go all the way with you?" Vincent quizzed me with the eagerness that only a seventeen-year-old, hormonally charged male attains. I didn't want to share the details, but I had to pacify his imagination for the moment.

"Sure, I mean, *eventually*, we went all the way." *How much of the truth should I tell him?* After all, Mrs. Emerson was still someone's neighbor, and I didn't want the rumor mill to grind out something embarrassing for her. "But it only happened once. I think it was more of an accident than anything on purpose, especially on her part." I figured I was responsible for some of it—I just looked older, bigger, and stronger than anyone else my age. Besides, my big brother had told my buddies and me about having sex with girls. In theory, we all thought it was pretty neat, but when it came down to the actual act,

I was nervous as a convict digging his way to freedom. I kept up the smoke-screen. "You know, Mrs. Emerson is a nice lady. She was just really lonely then, and after that one time, we were just friends."

"Sure you were, you dog! How come you got cut from study hall *every Thursday* then?" Vincent wasn't too swift in the academic department, but he did notice what was going on around him. He got in on a lot of action that way. But he wasn't going to learn the whole story about me and Mrs. Emerson.

"We never talked about it, but I could tell she didn't want me doing anything but yard work after that one day. And I respected her for that, because everyone has a weak moment here and there. So just drop it, Vincent. That's all there is to this story." I started talking about wrestling stats and thankfully Vincent let it go.

We finished our third beer just as we pulled into Belfry. We always stopped at the little café on our road trips to see if any chicks were hanging around looking for something to do.

"Kind of desolate tonight," Vincent remarked as he swung open the café door, the little bell tinkling against the glass.

A pimple-faced girl in her orange gingham waitress uniform appeared from the back room.

"Can I help you?" She stared at us behind her dark-rimmed glasses.

"Sure," I said. "How about a package of Juicy Fruit?"

As she turned back to the shelf behind the counter, I admired the way her uniform pulled tight to the roundness of her backside.

"I'll have a Hershey Bar," said Vincent. "Where is everybody tonight?"

"There's a calf roping in Joliet."

"Are you going?" Vincent leered into her over the counter.

"No, I have to stay here and close at ten, so it's not worth it for me 'cause it would be over by then."

"Too bad you have to stay in this hole all night. We're heading to Red Lodge—heard there was a dance at the high school."

We paid her and left. I looked at my watch before getting behind the wheel.

"We're making good time. We should be there just past seven thirty. Get me another beer."

We sped up the small valley past Bear Creek. Sooty smears marked the hillside where the coal had been dug up. The buildings were crumbling now, abandoned since the railroad had closed years earlier.

"Wasn't there an explosion in the mine?" Vincent glanced at the junked and rusted pickups piled and forgotten in the gullies.

"Yeah, I guess it was the Smith mine, and seventy-some men died in it."

"Sure looks like just an old ghost town now, huh?" We both clammed up then, lost in our own thoughts.

Maybe it was the stories my mom told, or maybe it was the faint memory of watching my grandparents stumble up the driveway at dusk to deliver the news, but at that moment, I felt the presence of my dad hovering over us. He'd lost his life almost to the day thirteen years ago. Squeezing my eyes to stop the threatening tears, I stepped on the gas and we ran the Chevy silently up the small pass and into Red Lodge in record time, just twelve minutes from Belfry.

It was almost dusk when we coasted into town and past the motels on the south end of Main. Ski season was over, so this part of town was dead. We turned north onto the main drag and geared down to a stealthy pace to ogle girls strolling down the sidewalks.

For a half hour we drove to the end of Main Street, looped through a vacant gas station, and back up the street. We finally managed to get behind two chicks and follow them to the vacant lot at the gas station. I laid on the horn and Vincent waved them over. They pulled up beside us. Their car was just as impressive as the girls — a white Ford Mustang, probably less than a year old. I noticed the chrome fender badge, so I knew it had the big 289 engine.

"Must be Papa's car," I whispered to Vincent as he rolled down his window.

The blonde in the driver's seat sported a tight gold sweater under a light blue ski coat. Her eyes matched the coat, and her full lips were glossy with some kind of lipstick. Her shoulder-length hair framed her slim face. I couldn't see anything below her shoulders, but my mind flashed a naked vision of her.

We had a good look at the other girl too. She was definitely cute, a Kelly-green sweater showing off her full breasts. Vincent looked at me and gave me the thumbs up.

"Hi, I'm Vincent and this is Will. We're from Cody. We're wondering if there's a dance tonight."

"I'm Pam," said the blonde, "and this is Rhonda. There is a dance — it's at the Moose Hall — starts at nine."

I nudged Vincent's side. "It's only eight thirty. Ask them if they want to ride around and have a beer with us."

The girls moved their car to the rear of the gas station and parked. When they hopped out, bending over to grab their purses, we both noticed how firm their thighs and hips were under skin-tight jeans. As the brunette slid in beside me, all I could see was her green sweater pulled taut over large, protruding breasts.

The next half hour turned into the usual question-and-answer session.

"How often do you come to Red Lodge," they asked. "Do you ski? Is this your car, Will? What grade are you in?"

We boldly answered each question, anticipating a make-out session if we were suave and sophisticated enough to impress them.

"What's your favorite band? Do you go to all the dances? Is that Mustang your dad's car? Where do you live?"

Rhonda answered our last question by guiding us onto a side street to a section of town that was dominated by newly built houses.

"Is that *your* house?" I asked. It was the largest home on the block, with a two-story brick fireplace, big windows, and a two-stall garage. "What does your dad do for a living?"

"He owns the lumber yard and built most of our house himself."

"That's cool. It must be great to live in such a beautiful home." I hoped Rhonda would never come to Cody and see our puny yellow duplex with its chipped siding. I couldn't wait to get out of her neighborhood and back to more comfortable turf. This girl was way out of my league.

Leaving her neighborhood, we cruised along Main and then drove through the parking lot at the dance hall. Couples filed through a wooden door in the side of the huge stone building. Rhonda mentioned that the band must be playing by now, so I parked the car in a dark corner of the lot. The girls looped their hands through our arms as we walked, giggling with anticipation of their grand entrance with the cool guys from Cody. The door hinges squeaked in front of us as we climbed the grimy steps. Inside, we turned in to a small lobby with a coat room. The dusty green walls held up the high ceiling and echoed our voices as we bought four tickets. The girls hung up their coats and we walked into the dark gallery. We fell into a natural couple's pattern, me with Rhonda, Vincent with Pam. After a few dances, we began skipping out to the car for drinks and some backseat action.

Around eleven o'clock, I met Vincent in the restroom. "Let's take off with the girls," I said, and Vincent agreed—it was time to blow this Popsicle stand.

What seemed so logical to us was met with some resistance from Rhonda and Pam.

"We're having fun—aren't you?"

"The band is great—let's stay and dance some more."

We had to think fast to quell their objections. "Yeah, they're groovy! We just want to go for a spin and get some fresh air. We'll be back before they play their last set." Vincent was a master of persuasion. He should be—he'd had plenty of practice in that category.

"Well, okay," Rhonda said cautiously. "But just make sure you get us back here before they're done for the night. My parents would shoot me if they knew I left the dance."

Pam nodded her agreement. We set our mental stopwatches, hoping that our hormones wouldn't wipe out all common sense.

We zigzagged up the canyon onto the switchbacks from Red Lodge. As we pulled into the deserted campground, more chitchat took place. We coasted into an open meadow, claiming that star gazing was on the menu. Vincent killed the motor but left the radio on. Lucky for us, the girls started swooning over Tom Jones belting out "What's New Pussycat?" You could count on Tom to set the mood for a make-out session. For no reason my mom's voice popped into my brain: "*He's a reckless driver! Don't go with Vincent. If you go anywhere, you drive the car. Don't let him get behind the wheel.*" But the beer and the heavenly scent of the girl sitting beside me in the backseat drowned out the words.

Rhonda had already slipped over to my side of the backseat, nestling under my arm. Her giggle was contagious, and her delicate arms captured my imagination as she slipped them around my chest. Confident that I could coax the sexual tide out of my ripe young date, I used my best move. I knew she would swing between passion and restraint, pulled back and forth like a weighted pendulum. I wrapped my hand around her waist, pulling her with a brisk tug but not so fast as to cause alarm. Cupping my hand under her chin, I eased her eager face up until we locked eyes. I took my time, savored the moment. Intoxicated by her warm, soft skin and willing lips, I readied myself for contact. We kissed, but not before Christine's smile slammed me between the eyes. I bungled it and we ended up in an awkward sort of head-butt position. I jerked away, instinctively glancing out the back window.

How could I do this to Christine? I broke into a full-bodied sweat.

"Are you okay, Will?" Rhonda pulled on my shirt sleeve.

"Uh, sure. No problem, I thought I heard a bobcat in the bushes. It must have just been Vincent's heavy breathing." Rhonda giggled and snuggled back under my arm.

A scuffle from the front seat got our attention. We could hear Vincent groping Pam, trying to pull her closer to him. "Vincent, slow down! We're not in a race here, you know," she whispered loud enough for us to hear. Vincent ignored us and brushed off Pam's objections.

"Vincent, you're a jerk! Take us back to the dance. *Now!*" Pam plastered herself against the passenger side door and stared out the window.

"Huh. Well, you sure led me to believe *you* wanted what *I* wanted," Vincent huffed, turning the key and slamming the Chevy into first gear, then grinding it into a fast second. Gravel pummeled the car's underbelly when he rounded the corner to get out of the campground. We swung around the turn and I felt the rear end dip as the back tire slid into the weeds.

"Slow down, asshole! Don't tear the oil pan out or we'll never get back to town!"

WILL: MIRAGE

Do not dwell in the past, do not dream of the future,
concentrate the mind on the present moment.

— Buddha

Remembering that awful night had thrown me into a loathing trance. Shaking my head, I found myself staring at Mom in the hospital room.

I don't know how much time went by — probably minutes — but it felt like hours. Finally, Mom gathered her sweater to her chest, pulled out her last tissue from her sleeve, and dabbed at her nose and eyes.

"Will, you know we aren't much for religion and we don't ever go to church. But this might be a good time for both of us to pray. It's the only thing I know to do right now."

She didn't know any prayers by heart, so she said something like, "Dear God, if it's Your will, please let my son live. He's a good boy, and he has a lot of living left to do. Lord, we need You today to help us be strong."

I was not at all eager to pray. *God?! Damn You! You put me in this predicament. Why should I ask for Your help?* Guilt took over then. *Why should God even listen to me, a fugitive from His church?* Respect for Mom and her attempt to comfort me finally won out. I croaked out a few words.

"God, please don't let my mom's heart break. I know I'm a sinner and you have no reason to let me live. But for her sake, please show me what I'm supposed to do next. And, God—if I am going to die, please let me see my brothers and my little sister one more time."

My mom already had that in the works and had convinced the charge nurse to let my brother Gordy in to see me—he was allowed to come in twice and I saw my baby sister once.

Mom told me that my older brother Dean was trying to get an emergency pass from Bangor's branch chief, Master Sergeant Gill, to fly stand-by and get home to see me. I knew I'd have to live for a few more days if I wanted to see him. By the time I saw my brother, my condition had stabilized. He stayed with me in my room almost round the clock for a whole week.

This really perked me up. My big brother took my mind off my troubles. We talked about fishing, chasing girls, car repairs, and playing ball.

He complained about the base commander who put

him on working nights, long shifts of twelve to sixteen hours. After they switched him to days, he liked it better and he even joined the air base's softball team.

"Last week, we beat the 'Transpo' unit, twenty-five to sixteen," he boasted. "And after a couple of cans of cool Colt 45, I felt pretty good!"

We spent hours reminiscing about growing up together, about racing cars and comparing notes about girls. He told me all about a girl named Charley he'd met at John and Mary's Booze Soak.

"Her real name is Charlene. She's about two inches shorter than me and has a great body. She water skis and her father owns a cottage and boat. So you know what I'll be doing most of the summer."

"What else besides chasing this girl are you doing up there in Maine?" I asked.

"Things are swell in Bangor," he said. "The weather finally broke and I went fishing with Sergeant Monte once."

He told me how he'd bought a rod and reel for fifteen dollars at the base general store that would've cost thirty in town.

"We caught all kinds of perch that were about eight to fourteen inches long, and some chubs, which aren't any good. They're like suckers. Sarge caught one sucker and a trout that was about twelve inches. I haven't caught any trout yet, but I've been trying with that new rod."

"Makes my mouth water," I said, "thinking about a

fresh trout dinner. Remember how we used to use our knives to filet them, roll them in corn meal, and roast them over our campfire?"

"Boy, do I," said Dean. "When you get out of this place, you'll have to come visit me in Maine. We'll go to this great spot and throw our lines in, try our luck."

I smiled. My first smile since the accident. His positive attitude that everything would be back to normal in a short time boosted my spirits and gave me the will to go on living.

After my brother left, things got boring. I counted dots on the ceiling until I was sick of it. At first I couldn't sit up in bed without passing out or throwing up. My nurses were the only bright spot in those long, drawn-out days.

In 1966, most hospitals didn't have Intensive Care Units as such, so the nursing supervisors and the bigwigs in administration allowed two student nurses to develop and implement their first ICU, with me as their first intensive care patient. In addition to my two nurses Kathy and Jan, there was Judy—a nurse's aide—who'd been assigned to stay in my room for her entire shift from the time I landed in the hospital. Judy did a damn good job, considering she had only worked for three days as an aide before I got there.

This damned accident turned my life upside down. I'd already made plans and knew what I wanted to do after graduation. By May that year, the Vietnam War started to escalate. A bunch of friends my brother's age had already been drafted and fought in the infantry. Two of my very close buddies were sent back in body bags. I was terrified, sure that I'd get drafted. I didn't want to get shot at or killed. I came up with a plan to avoid the draft. My dad had been in the Navy's "CB" program — the Construction Builders. In the fall of my junior year, I'd contacted a heavy equipment school in Idaho and got the information to take to our banker. The loan officer told me to come see him the day after graduation and he'd approve the school loan. I knew I could get a draft exemption for being in school; eventually I'd have to sign up, though, so my plan was to enlist in the Navy CB's. If I got accepted there, I figured I'd probably not end up in the middle of the fighting even if I was sent to Nam.

Now, stuck in this hospital bed, I couldn't put my plan into motion—I couldn't do *anything* I used to do. Except tell jokes. My nurses were all young, attractive, intelligent girls. They liked my teasing and teased me back. But I could tell that Judy was scared as hell about her assignment of taking care of me. I tried going easier on her with the teasing, and she seemed to relax after a while. Then I got a roommate.

When it was time for the tongs to come out, I was no longer considered an intensive care patient, so they set me up for a two-bed room. When they wheeled Byron in from his elbow surgery, I chuckled. He happened to be a Cody High friend, and we started right in on the nurses.

For those two weeks, we teased Judy until she couldn't take it anymore. We found out she'd asked to be transferred. Guilt set in; I asked Jan to please ask Judy to come see me one more time. When she walked in the room, I turned beet red.

"Judy, I'm really sorry. I promise we won't tease you anymore. Just come back and be our nurse. You're really good at it, and we need you here."

Byron nodded enthusiastically. "Yeah, you're the best!"

After that, we just had some good laughs and I warned Byron to behave himself around Judy.

With his elbow on the mend, Byron was released and went back home. After the time with my roommate and reminiscing about school life, I swore to myself that I would never return to Cody unless I was back to my old self before the injury. I was going to walk again. I would do all those things that a normal seventeen-year-old guy does. I'd had some broken bones and injuries before this neck incident. I knew recovery would take some time and a lot of work. The neurosurgeons confirmed it. According to them, there should be no reason that, after some months in a rehabilitation unit, I couldn't walk out with little or no limitations at all. It made sense to me. Besides, the trusted experts should know. Right!?!

I didn't want any of my friends to see me with my Frankenstein tongs, or even the "four-poster" brace once the tongs were taken out of my skull. But they came to the hospital to see me anyway. I'd been running a fever and the summer days were heating up, so the nurses covered my waist with a towel and left the rest of my body naked. They'd run a couple of electric fans when they bathed me, using water cooled with ice.

This particular June day was hot, nearing ninety degrees, so Kathy had left the fans running after my bath. I was flat on the bed, counting the dots in the ceiling for the umpteenth time, not thinking of much of anything. I heard a shuffle outside my door but couldn't turn my head to see who it was. I heard the footsteps coming nearer. I knew it was a girl, because the sound was like my nurses' feet and I could tell the difference. Men's feet would thump, and I could feel the vibration coming up from the floor through the metal railings on my bed.

When my mysterious visitor neared the bed, the fan blew my towel off, exposing my genitals. I didn't know what a catheter looked like, but an orderly had described it to me once—I knew it was grotesque. Pauline (I was finally able to see her face) kept her cool, picking up the towel and covering me. Not embarrassed in the least, she struck up the conversation and we ended up talking all afternoon. Pauline was one of my best friends. More times than not, it was me, Gordy, and her hanging out together, running out to Red Lake for parties, or out to the dam to watch midnight dragsters blow through the tunnel, or getting Cokes and fries at the Geyser drive-in.

She filled me in on all the guys who went into the

service right away after graduation, all the girls who got married or the unmarried ones who went to Powell to learn shorthand for their future secretarial jobs. We joked around and laughed about some of our silly classmates and their antics. It was good to have my friend with me again. It was also really painful. Homesickness washed over me, stifling our conversation. She got up to leave, leaned over, and kissed me square on the mouth—a long, tender kiss—then leaned back, her gaze intent upon my face.

"Will, you'll get out of here and you'll be back with us very soon, I know it. If anybody can whip this 'paralyzed' thing, you can. And I can speak for me and all of our friends: We'll be there for you when you do come back home. I promise."

She smiled at me, but I saw the hope and the pain behind her eyes. She turned, and her footsteps receded into the hall and out of hearing. Alone again with my thoughts.

I'm not normal anymore and I won't ever be normal again.

After that, when anyone except my family came to visit, I'd ask the nurses to tell them I was meeting with my doctor, or sleeping, or sick—anything to avoid seeing my old school friends. I quit returning phone calls or answering letters. A couple of the hospital volunteers offered to write them for me, but I refused.

The days dragged into weeks in that dismal infirmary. At first, flowers in vases still showed up, and the cards were arranged around the room so I could see them from the bed. Eventually, the flowers withered into miniature skeletons, turning into graphic announcements of my despondent thoughts. The cards were taken off the windowsills, stashed into drawers, and coffined out of sight. Even the summer sun streaming through my window late into the afternoon wouldn't clear away my oppressive gloom.

My only visitor was Mom. She drove up from Cody every Wednesday afternoon. Her boss would let her have the time off as long as she worked Saturday mornings to make up the time. *Asshole!*

She'd stay late on Wednesday nights, thankfully until I fell asleep, then drive back home alone. She'd come back up on Sundays, too, and stay all day. I counted the hours from Wednesday to Sunday. My little brother Gordy couldn't come with her much; he was working at the Irma Hotel and had to work evenings and weekends. He was only fourteen, and he more or less took care of himself when Mom was gone. Janie was already in Colorado for the summer with Grandpa and Grandma, so Mom didn't have to worry what to do with my ten-year-old sister.

I had lots of time to think between her visits. I'd given up trying to piece together the night of the accident; it was too hard to think about the "if onlys" and how the night would have turned out different. *If only* I had driven from the campground, knowing that Vincent had drank too much already. *If only* we had stayed at the game in Cody that night instead of heading to Red Lodge. *If only* we hadn't met up with the girls and they hadn't agreed to go with us that night.

I took to staring moodily at my legs. They'd lost the sharp, agonizing pains I had experienced right after the wreck. In fact, the lack of feeling in my feet and legs seemed almost pleasant now. It was like I was cut off from my chest down. I would look down at them and think, *Those legs belong to someone else.* I didn't care anymore.

On most days I was so lethargic, I just wanted to go to sleep and not ever wake up. If I could have done it, I would have curled up in a ball—pulled my knees up close and pushed my head down, in the fetal position—and welcomed death. It would be so much better than these endless hours in this vault they called a hospital room.

I knew it was getting close to the Fourth of July because the nurses were talking about who was going to get the weekend off and who had to pull extra shifts at work. What did I care? I wouldn't be shooting any fireworks off this year, no hanging out with my friends and drinking beer, our favorite pastime.

I started writing my obituary in my head.

"William Walter Alves, born February 17, 1949—died July 4, 1966. He was a lovable guy from Colorado. At seventeen, he got dealt a rotten hand at the height of his manhood. Died a slow death after a car wreck. Survived by his mom,

two brothers, a sister, grandparents, and assorted stepdads. Preceded in death by his father, Everett Alves."

Then, I thought I really *was* going to die. I started getting real sick. Something was seriously wrong with my body, but I couldn't feel anything below my collar bone. I had fever and chills, sweating one minute and shivering the next. I couldn't keep any food down. I drank water or liquids constantly to keep my mouth and throat wet. The nurses started a drip again just so I wouldn't get dehydrated. Mom showed up for one of her Wednesday visits, and as soon as she walked in the room, she saw how far gone I was. She went and found the doctor right away.

He told her there was nothing more they could do for me and wanted me out of the hospital by the end of the week. We both knew that quack doctor didn't know what was wrong with me; he just wanted me gone before I kicked the bucket on his watch.

Scared to die, and afraid to be so sick and live, I tormented myself with suicidal thoughts. I told Mom, "It's okay, I'm ready to die. What do I have to live for anyway?"

"William Walter, don't you *ever* say that again!"

I'd never seen her so furious.

"You may have a broken body, but you still have your mind and you're a smart boy, smarter than most. You have me and we'll get this figured out somehow."

And she did. Right away, she started making phone calls. She knew we had to act fast, that we didn't have much time before whatever was attacking my body would take over and do me in.

She found a way to get me to the rehabilitation center in Thermopolis, Wyoming, nearly two hundred miles away. I knew she couldn't afford to have the ambulance take me all that way. It was no easy task to transport me, a paralyzed cripple. I couldn't just hop into a car seat and go. As sick as I was, my curiosity still got the better of me.

When she got back to my room, I asked her, "Mom, how in the hell am I going to get all the way to Thermopolis like this?"

"Well, honey, I talked to an acquaintance of mine in Cody. Now, don't get alarmed. He's the mortician there, but he's agreed to come up here. We'll use his hearse and it'll be perfect for moving you on a gurney in the back of it."

"A hearse! You've got to be kidding me! Now I *know* I'm dying."

"For God's sake, Will, stop that! We're going to get you there and get you some help. You just hang in there, honey."

Three hours later, I lay on a gurney, staring up at the tufted satin ceiling of the hearse, a baby blue sound chamber. The sliding window between me and the front seat was closed and I was completely sealed in, insulated from the outside world. At first I panicked. What if I quit breathing back here? They wouldn't have a clue. I couldn't alert them that something was wrong. I panicked. *I'm entombed!* Then Mom slid the window open and asked if I was comfortable, that she was right there if I needed anything. After that I drifted in and out of sleep and sweat, listening to the drone of the tires on the highway and their muted voices talking about how long they thought it would take to get there.

They rushed me to intake the moment we arrived. After some brief tests, the doctor called my mom into the examination room. Dr. Reed told us that my pituitary gland was injured. He explained that it was causing problems with my blood pressure, glucose levels, regulation of my metabolism, and my kidneys were also shutting down.

He could give me an injection to try to reactivate the pituitary gland, he said, and if I made it through the night, I would probably live. Otherwise, he doubted I would make it at all.

At that point, the mortician didn't want to wait around anymore; he wanted to get back to Cody. So I got the shot and, having no other choice, Mom took off for Cody in the hearse. As soon as the mortician dropped her off at the house, she hopped in the car and drove back down here. She got to the rehab center around three in the morning.

My condition had started to improve, and the nurses encouraged her to get some sleep. She stayed by my side the entire night, and each time the pain spasms woke me, she was there to mop the sweat off my forehead and whisper that we'd get through this together.

BEVERLY: QUANDARY

Mothers are the necessity of invention.

— Bill Watterson

There's a room inside the Goetche Rehab Center in Thermopolis that's used for families when they're told a loved one has passed away. I know this because I was there with my cousin Margaret in 1962 when they called her there to tell her that her husband had died.

In July of 1966, I found myself in that room again. When the Cody mortician and I pulled into the center's driveway near midnight, my only thought was to get Will inside and have the doctor examine him.

Will's condition had gone downhill in the week before they released him from the hospital in Billings. He was running a high fever, and his skin was clammy and cold as we drove him the two hundred miles to Thermopolis that night.

When Dr. Reed came in and saw him, he immediately ordered the nurses to bring him a syringe full of some type of substance. He recognized right away what he needed to do to revive Will. I had faith that this doctor knew exactly what he was doing. The next moment demolished my hopes. Dr. Reed bowed slightly so he was at eye level with me.

"Please understand, Mrs. Alves. We're going to try this, but I don't know if he will make it through the night."

WILL: NURSES

Modesty? Please! I am a nurse. I have seen more privates than an army general.

— Unknown

It was mid-July 1966 and I was officially in "rehab" at Goettche Center in Thermopolis, Wyoming. With any mention of "rehabilitation" and "physical therapy," I heard "get me back to normal." When Dr. Schwimmer discharged me from the hospital in Billings, he told my mom that I'd be soon fitted with leg braces and crutches and would probably walk out of the rehab center in six to eight months. She was beaming when she told me what he said, filling us both with hope and confidence.

The long rehabilitation process began. First, we had to get my body adjusted to being elevated again, since I'd been lying flat for two months. For the first week, the nurses would transfer me from my hospital bed onto a wheeled car to transport me to the physical therapy room. For an hour each morning and another hour each afternoon, I was strapped to a "tilt table." The motorized platform stood me up to ninety degrees to help my body adjust to bearing weight and pressure. The therapist started me out at a twenty-degree angle for a couple of days; then to forty-five degrees for a few more days; and finally upright to ninety degrees. After I could stand at that angle for a couple of days and not pass out, I graduated to a wheelchair. It was early August—I'd passed the tilt table test sooner than they expected and now could propel myself in my wheelchair.

At this rate, I'll be able to wrestle by January. This is real progress now!

I expected any day to be fitted for leg braces and receive a pair of crutches. Then I realized I had very little movement of my arms. The therapist had been moving and stretching my arms every day since I'd arrived and I'd sensed tingling in my biceps and forearms.

They're just waiting until I can strengthen and use my arms before getting me up on my feet.

At least a month went by, with daily therapy, before I could lift only a quarter pound of weight. About every three days after that, the weight was increased until I could move my arms enough to lift my hand up to my mouth.

Oh, boy! I can finally feed myself! No more teaspoonfuls of diced food, then waiting nearly fifteen minutes at times before getting another bite. My fingers were still numb. *How the hell am I going to get a grip on a fork?*

"No problem," said my occupational therapist. First, we tried a utensil with a bulky, built-up handle, but it was so heavy when I loaded it with food, it fell out of my "no grip" hand. Next, we tried elastic-lined cuffs that slipped over my hand and had a little pocket for the utensil handle to slide into. This method resulted in as much food on my ring finger and little fingers as there was on the fork. Feeling like a messy toddler, my anger and frustration boiled over. I still couldn't feed myself. After one such exasperating feeding session, I asked my nurse to bring me five or six rubber bands in different sizes. I stretched and twisted the rubber bands this way and that around my fingers for about an hour. I hit on a method of holding my two middle fingers together tight enough to hold a utensil and not get my fingers in the food when I scooped it up. Cindy, my therapist, was impressed with my invention. She and the others in the therapy department eventually devised a hand brace constructed of metal plates for my fingers and leather straps instead of the rubber bands. I began eating like a man again.

For the rest of the summer, I used my brace to learn the basics of other daily tasks as a quadriplegic, like brushing my teeth and writing. I gained more movement in my arms and started building my strength in those muscles. The therapists were still coming to my room and wheeling me through the sanitized hallway to the therapy room to practice my exercises and all the torture that went along with "rehabilitation."

"Come on, Will. You can wheel across the room. Keep your arm strength up. By the time you get back to Cody, you can challenge any bozo on the basketball team to a race down the court!" My therapist, Cindy, was a cute brunette with a fiery attitude. I was in love with her. She didn't have a clue that I'd been rolling around the place in my chair when no one was around. I knew I could wheel at least ten feet before giving out. I faked that I was tired and needed to go back to my room. On the way back, we were passing the Hubbard Tank room when an orderly called for her to help him get a patient out of the tank. She left me in the hallway, and the door closed behind her as she stepped into the room. I spotted an open door a few feet in front of me. Wheeling frantically toward it, I knew I had only a minute before she'd be back in the hallway. I rolled through the door and around the door jamb, disappearing from the line of sight that she'd have when she walked out of the Hubbard room. It would have been funnier if I could have seen the look on her face when she realized she'd "lost" her patient!

Did I mention how much I loved my nurses? Especially Margo—petite, big-chested Margo with a big smile for me every day. She was also in charge of my bowel program. Which caused me a lot of anxiety at first. I would have never dreamed that my first exotic sexual experience would involve a rehab nurse performing "dillies" on me. I already knew the routine of rolling me onto my side, tucking a Chux under my backside, inserting the suppository, anchoring the bedpan against my butt, and waiting fifteen minutes for the magic to happen. Margo turned me on to the added thrill of doing dillies on me. She'd come into my room at the prescribed fifteen minutes, put on the latex gloves, lube up her index finger with K-Y Jelly, and then the fun began. Dillies are slow, rotating motions around the inside rectum wall to stimulate the anus and allow reflexes to open the orifice so the stool can move out easier. Margo joked around a lot during our routine; she made me laugh and took my mind off the process taking place behind me. She knew when distress would hit me, so she'd come around front to massage my stomach. I couldn't feel it, but I could see the gentle compassion in her eyes. The most amazing eyes I'd ever come across — deep golden with specks of iridescent brown — I called them tiger eyes and she loved it. She'd finish up, soothing me with warm washcloths and a flannel blanket around my shoulders. Then she'd bring me a not-too-hot cup of Tang and two aspirin.

"Sweet dreams, my handsome man." She'd wink at me as she left to continue on her rounds.

Smiling, I thought about the joke on myself. Who would have thought that my life at seventeen years old would include a gorgeous nurse and kinky sex?

WILL: SCHOOL DAYS

Hope is like a bird that senses the dawn and
carefully starts to sing while it is still dark.

— Anonymous

By the time fall quarter started at Hot Springs County High, Cindy and the other therapists had devised a way for me to go to school. They'd figured out how to use a pair of loudspeakers to communicate with the classrooms. I had one speaker and the teachers had the other one. From my room at the rehab center, I was able to "sit in" on classes. The trickiest part for the teachers was making sure that a student would haul the loudspeaker to my next period. Since I couldn't write fast enough with my dead fingers to keep up on assignments, some of the kids came over after school to take dictation from me and write my papers. That was the highlight of my day. A couple of the guys would blast into my room with reams of papers from the teachers, and the girls would show up on a regular basis too. Cute ones like Twink Sherwood and Linda Brooks would stop in two or three times a week. Jolene Zupan or the Swedish exchange student Eva Wersall would come by on the weekends too. I suspected I was the excuse to get the girls to come, just so they could flirt with them instead of doing homework. I found myself in a precarious position. I needed the boys to bring me homework, but I was the one who charmed the girls. Since I needed male allies to help me get assignments done, I worked on making friends with them.

My two best buddies were Jim Wilson and Gary Brost. All of us had come off the ranches and had a lot in common when it came to rodeo talk, or spring calving, or putting up hay. We'd start shooting the breeze about how we'd go around and put up hay and straw for other ranchers, and at the end of the day, we'd always end up in the shop with the other hired help, leaning on a truck bumper, listening to the stories about dating the girls from town. We all agreed that ranches and farms are amazing for dates; you can walk to the far side of a moonlit field, lie in the grass, and show them the stars.

About three months into the school year, I kept getting a pressure sore at the base of my spine and I couldn't sit in my chair or even lie on my back at night. I had another sore on my butt cheek that was giving me fits too. In order to let the sores heal, I needed to be on my stomach several hours a day. Jim and Gary and I talked about it one day after school.

"Hey, guys. I just wanted to let you know I might have to drop out of school this semester."

"What? Why?" Jim and Gary looked at each other, wide-eyed.

"I mean, I know you've been struggling with getting assignments done lately," Gary said, looking over at Jim again. "But it's no different for us, with football and trying to keep up on classes too."

"It's embarrassing to talk about, really," I said. "But, basically, the doc told me I can't sit in my chair so many hours a day—I'm going to have to be in bed most of the time."

"Why? What's going on?" Jim was restless now, sidling over to sit on the windowsill.

"I have sores on my butt. That's the *Reader's Digest* version," I said.

"So what? Who doesn't get butt sore once in a while," Gary said, making a sort of grumbling in his throat. He shot another glance at Jim, then me, a faint smile building in the corners of his mouth.

We all cracked up and in between chuckles and snorts, we started talking about "what if?" and "there must be something we can figure out," and "you can't drop out now, Will. We're counting on you to fill in on our basketball team the first of the year."

"Hey, you know what?" said Jim. "I saw this piece of equipment once, when my dad and I were in Denver at the hospital. We were visiting my grandma; she was real sick, and my dad said we should go see her, just in case — you know, in case she didn't make it."

"Okay...what was this thing you saw?" My tone of voice gave away my skepticism.

"It was like a gurney they use in the ambulances, and it had wheels. There were these armrests stuck out the sides of it, and it had like a round donut hole at one end."

Gary and I exchanged glances. Jim continued his story.

"I'd gotten bored with sitting there in the room with my dad and grandma, and had wandered downstairs to find a vending machine for some candy. I stumbled into their physical therapy room and saw this thing. One of the therapists came up behind me, and I just about jumped out of my skin when he said 'hi' to me. He explained that it was for paralyzed people to lay on facedown, and a person could rest their head in the donut hole."

Gary twirled his finger around his head. Cuckoo was his diagnosis for Jim's condition.

"Jim, you might have something," I said. If there was some way I could lie on my stomach but still be mobile, maybe I could still do my assignments and keep up in school. My excitement was short-lived when I thought about the cost.

"My mom can't afford to buy medical equipment that's being built overseas in Europe," I said, remembering what the therapist had explained to Jim that day in the Denver hospital.

"We can build it ourselves," Jim said. "In the shop at school."

"Really? You think so?"

"Yeah. Let me draw it for you — where's your paper and pencils?" Jim rummaged around on the desk and started sketching out was to become known as my surfboard.

We talked the shop teacher into letting my buddies assemble a sturdy wooden platform that attached to my wheelchair. Mr. Harding delivered it himself, beaming as he wheeled it into my room with the physical therapists on his heels. They were all excited and helped transfer me to the board right then and there.

There were two parts to the platform: The top piece lay horizontally from the back of the wheelchair and rested above the seat. The other piece angled from above the seat to the footrests in the front of the chair. Instead of sitting in the chair, I was suspended above it with my head extended past the back of the chair. The platform had a cut-out for my face, and a canvas strap was attached to the frame so that I could rest my forehead on it.

The surfboard was cool because I could still get around anywhere in the rehab unit while I was strapped to it. I could reach the rear wheels with my hands and motor around that way. I could wheel myself to the table to read and do homework or even eat dinner. The surfboard was a big hit and for a couple of weeks, a parade of visitors filled the hallways of the rehab center.

I didn't have to drop out of school after all. The weeks flew by with studies and therapy and goofing around with Gary and Jim after school. I was part of the school scene again. My photo showed up in the school annual. The senior class secretary delivered a freshly printed copy to me with wishes from the entire student council. As I flipped through the pages of the annual, I saw that Cheryl (I had a crush on her) Richardson and I were crowned as the two students with the "Most Endurance." The caption read, "The sky's the limit when Will and Cheryl set out to achieve a goal." Another photo, taken of me in my room at the rehabilitation center, showed me with an open book and pressing the button on the loudspeaker. This caption read, "Will Alves, former Cody student, listens in on one of his four classes which he was enrolled in the first semester at HSCHS."

I didn't want to leave Thermopolis. But the gears were already grinding to release me from the rehabilitation center.

Doctor Reed said I was ready to go home. It was the second time I heard that there was nothing more they could do for me. This was as good as it was going to get.

"But, Doc, I'm not ready to go yet. There have been other cripples like me that got feeling back and can walk again," I argued. "In fact, I think my right hand is getting better. I can feel more tingling in it each day."

"Will, the people you've read about didn't have their

spinal cords severed all the way like yours. Theirs grew back together and allowed the nerves to function again. This isn't the case with you. I'm sorry."

I'd been faithfully doing everything they wanted me to in physical therapy. I'd convinced myself I was going to walk again. All those false hopes that had kept me going all those months disappeared in that moment like smoke into thin air. Uncontrollable tears welled up; I turned my head away but the doctor had noticed.

Dr. Reed laid his hand on my shoulder.

"Will." His voice was low and soft. "How about if you stay here until January when the mid-point of the school year is over?"

"Sure, that sounds swell," I said. But it wasn't swell at all. My world was turning upside down again.

I finally accepted that I'd have to make plans to go back to Cody. Just so we could see what we were up against, Mom brought me home one weekend. Gordy came with her that time. It was kind of scary for me to get in a car again because there wasn't any way to strap me down—we didn't have seat belts then. I worried about riding in the car for the first time (well, since the first ride in the hearse) when riding home from Thermopolis to Cody.

The orderlies helped get me into the front seat of the car at Thermopolis, and when I got home, my brother and Mom got me into the house.

I slept in Mom's bed because it was on the main floor

of the two-story duplex. But it was hard for them to get me up and down. There was no equipment there to help out — no hospital bed, no hydraulic lift, nothing mechanical like they had at Thermopolis.

I got embarrassed, too, because of all the things they had to do for me and my care — empty the piss out of my leg bag, get me dressed and undressed, change the bandage on my ass to treat the bedsore. Thank God I wasn't due for my bowel movement program until I got back to the center. I wasn't very gracious in my role as household invalid. I yelled at them a lot that weekend. In a way, I couldn't wait to get back to rehab and the world I was relatively comfortable with after all those months.

Dr. Reed was really a good doctor, even though I figured I would have got a lot better if I would have been able to go to Denver for things like my bowel and urinary care. I'd read up on it some while I was sitting around the rehab center that summer. The doctors in Denver had progressed a lot with those things, but it seemed like Dr. Reed just did the basics. But I knew I couldn't push the point much with Mom, with finances so tight and all. So I did the next best thing. I learned about it myself as much as I could during my stay at the rehab center. I knew that when the time came, I could teach Mom and Gordy about it too.

The layout at the duplex wasn't going to work for us, so Mom had rented a house up on the hill, a log house, all on one floor. The furnace room was massive, so she had it fixed up for my bedroom, and even had a sink hooked up there. She'd found a used hospital bed, a portable lift, and a wheelchair. Along with those, she'd assembled the smaller things needed for my care — bedpan, catheter kit, and assorted drugstore items.

It was time to come home.

26

BEVERLY: NO ONE TO BLAME

A man loves his sweetheart the most,
his wife the best, but his mother the longest.

Irish Proverb

I didn't have a life. There were no prospects of a relationship. I had too much baggage. A paralyzed son. Other kids. What have you.

After a few years, I met Maggie Robertson. Like me, she'd been divorced for years. We got acquainted and started doing things together. She had a man friend for a while, but nothing ever came of it. I got bits and pieces of life that were separate from Will. But most of my time was absorbed by my son's needs and trying to keep it together for Gordy and Janie. I was exhausted, working at the office all week, doing my nursing duties every morning and every night, and trying to keep the household together. I had no relief from it.

I didn't know if I could sacrifice that much of myself to take care of my family. I swayed from guilt to resentment to hopelessness on a daily basis. I doubted my capacity to press on, day after day. I got so damn tired. Some nights when my head hit the pillow, I'd pray that I wouldn't wake up.

Will had a lot of frustrations in his life, too, early on. It wasn't just the big stuff, either. He was so particular about some things, like cleaning his eyeglasses. I'd be packing my lunch in the kitchen, getting my things ready to leave for the office.

"Mom, can you come here and clean my eyeglasses? They have smudges all over them," he'd call from the dining room table.

"Okay, but I have to leave for work in a few minutes," I'd remind him as I came into the room, reaching with both hands to pull them off his face.

I'd get the lens cleaner and cloth off the hall table, spray and wipe them, then repeat the process before navigating them back onto the bridge of his nose. He watched like a hawk the whole time. As soon as he had them on, inevitably came the next comment:

"Mom, there's a big smudge right in my line of sight on the left lens."

I'd start the process all over and clean them again, sometimes as many as four times.

At first, I was furious, stomping out the door and worried about being late, sure that the boss would yell at me. But then, I put myself in Will's shoes and realized he'd be there at home all day, sometimes alone for the entire day, without the ability to clean his own glasses. If he accidently touched the lens with his hand as he adjusted them, or if a splatter of food found its way onto his glasses, he had to tolerate it for hours until someone came home to help him.

I knew that I was witnessing the miracle of my son, who pressed on each day, who looked for the silver lining and didn't complain about the hardship of his condition. I didn't want to be so busy and distracted to notice. I was grateful to be part of his life experience. I learned patience. I accepted. I had been wrong to judge, and I learned about a thing called unconditional love.

I cannot remember why, but one night I was getting him to bed and we were really going at it. We were arguing and he was cussing and I was cussing, and here we were; we'd been yelling at each other for about an hour. Then we noticed Grandma standing in the doorway, tears streaming down her face. It was kind of funny to us. We just shut up and didn't say anything else the rest of the night. I think the argument was about him going back to school and that he needed to do something with his life. He'd been out of high school for a couple of years, and the business college hadn't worked out. He hadn't been doing anything but hanging around the house and sometimes going out in the green van if he could get Gordy or somebody else to take him somewhere.

The doctors tried to warn me about this part, telling me that it takes at least a few years for paralyzed people to accept their condition and start turning their lives around.

Many days Will would start talking about how he just knew he was going to get better, that the feeling in his fingers was increasing, that he thought he felt sensations in his legs.

"Maybe I'll walk again, Mom." He'd beam at me with that wide-open smile of his.

I'd have to hide out in my bedroom then so he wouldn't see my tears. I knew it wasn't going to happen but I didn't have the heart to tell him. He would never walk again.

BEVERLY: FULL OF PROMISE

I do not live on false promises.
I cannot afford to live on bad advice.

— Richard Kiyosaki

Will's accident left me full of promise. Every day brought promise — that is, promises I must make, promises I must make good on, every one of them. Yes, I will be at work today. No, I won't miss any more days this month; my son is living at home now. Even though he needs me each morning when he wakes up, and I'm the one to empty his leg bag that has swollen to bursting overnight. I'm the one to crank up the head of his hospital bed just so he can sit up. I'm the one who rearranges his blankets so he stays warm, who places his roller tray table in front of him so he can eat breakfast, who wraps rubber bands around his fingers so he can hold his spoon to feed himself. I must not forget to remove the rubber bands, lest his fingers swell and turn blue.

I promise to pay the medical bills, even though I have no idea where the money will come from or even if there will ever be any money to pay them.

I promise to…

WILL: HOMECOMING

Success is the sum of small efforts,
repeated day in and day out.

— Richard Collier

I was seventeen, six-foot-two, 220 pounds. She was forty, five-foot-four, 120 pounds. We were an unlikely pair. My severed spinal cord had brought us together in a way that most parents and kids don't ever experience. By day, she was the breadwinner, by night my nursemaid.

I was still the son, but with lifeless limbs, dead weight that had to be moved by someone else because I couldn't do it on my own. I was totally dependent on her strength and kindness to do the basic tasks of daily living for me. She was still the mom, but her days started much earlier than most people's because of me.

I'd hear her alarm ring around 5:00 a.m. and the shuffle of her slippers on the bare linoleum in the kitchen.

She'd quickly go to the bathroom, then to my room to start the ritual. We didn't have a lamp in the room, so she'd flick on the overhead light, jarring us both into a harsh wake-up call.

"Good morning, son," she'd say. "How did you sleep last night?"

"Okay until I heard the dogs bark next door. I've been awake for a while. How'd you sleep, Mom?"

"Oh, I slept so hard, I barely heard the alarm when it went off just now."

This was her usual reply to my usual question, as she pulled the cotton blanket down to me knees. She'd clamp off the tube to my leg bag (bloated from collecting a full night's worth of piss), disconnect it, and take the bag to the bathroom to empty it. Back again, she'd reconnect everything and check my catheter to make sure it hadn't loosened during the night. Tugging the covers back up around my chest, then moving to the end of my bed, she'd crank on the handle of the used hospital bed so I could sit upright.

Turning to the metal cabinet by my bed, she'd pull out the drawer, the metal guides whining against the steel drawer, to pick out the Dixie cup full of pills.

"I'll get fresh water," she said, picking up my large plastic cup with the lid and straw and taking it to the sink in my room. She'd arrange the 64-ouncer and pills neatly on the portable tray table and roll it into place over my lap. The large sippy cup always posed a problem for me. I knew I had to drink it to maintain my body functions, to stay healthy. But then, I had to rely on someone to empty the leg bag several times a day when it filled up with urine. I hated asking other people to do the deed. Who really wants to handle sixty-four ounces of someone else's smelly piss?

"I'll get breakfast started. Would you like hot cereal today?"

"Yes, Mom, that would be fine." Again, my usual answer to her usual question.

Breakfast was presented on a tray, like I was a guest in a fancy hotel, neatly arranged so I could pick up the toast with my "good" hand, the one with the most feeling. On my left hand, she'd strap on the brace, sliding the metal fingers with leather bands onto my hand and wrist, buckling the straps, adjusting them for my comfort. She'd place the spoon in my hand, helping wrap my fingers around it, and secure it tight with the brace. At last, I could begin the process of eating my oatmeal. By then it was cold and gooey. I didn't dare complain.

After clearing away the breakfast tray and pulling the portable tray table clear of the bed, she started my morning hygiene routine. She'd go get the steel washbasin full of warm water, bring soap and a washcloth, and give me a spit bath under my armpits and around my crotch area. It was necessary, I got that, but it was always a lesson in humility for me. Me, a macho man at seventeen, having my mom wash my crotch, handle my balls, and watch the uninvited boner spring up unannounced, but inevitable when detecting what it interpreted as fondling. Christ! Would the embarrassment ever end?

I took to making small talk while we performed our morning ritual. What was she doing at work that day? What were we doing for dinner? Was Gordy working tonight?

Tugging on the cotton blanket under my butt, she'd turn me on my side so she could dress the bedsore that showed up on a regular basis on at least one if not both of my butt cheeks. Cheerfully, she'd answer each of my questions.

"I have a big day; the auditors will be there to check my books." "I thought we'd fix pinto beans and ham for dinner. Janie can get it started for us when she gets home from school." "No, Gordy has tonight off." After she was done, with a firm pull on the blanket by her strong hands, I'd flop on my back like a rag doll weighted with lead.

Then we'd start the contortions needed to take off my pajamas and dress me. First, I'd lift my arms above my head, resting my forearms in the canvas slings dangling above the bed. She'd tug my T-shirt up over my shoulders and head, then pull my arms, one at a time, back down and out of the sleeve. She'd crank the bed back down flat, turning and tugging the pajama bottoms down from my waist, down my legs, then lift my feet, one at a time, to pull the PJs free of the dead clubs at the end of my legs. She'd reverse the steps to dress me. First, the underwear and pants, then the shirt. Button-ups were easier, but I didn't always want to wear the oxford shirts for every day.

Next was the process of getting me from the bed to the wheelchair. Using a chrome and canvas lift on wheels, she secured the straps around my butt, used the lift to swing me from bed to chair, then lower me into the chair. After pulling on my socks, wriggling my shoes into place, she was always so gentle when she picked my feet up and put them on the foot pedals of the chair.

One last adjustment to pull my shirt down in back because it would always ride up on me in the canvas lift. She combed my hair, and tenderly cleaned my eyeglasses one more time. They seemed to get smudged so easily these days. The tedious two-hour daily ritual was complete.

"You are looking particularly handsome today," she'd chirp as she turned to walk out of my room.

Mom worked, of course, during the day while I went to school. We had to figure out a way to get my home care set up. Right away, Mom got a lady to come in during the day, but she didn't have enough money to pay her, so some people at her work said to go to the welfare office.

She took my little sister Janie with her to talk to the welfare man. She explained our situation. We were still waiting to hear about the insurance settlement, which had dragged on for months.

"He just hemmed and hawed and finally told us, 'I just can't help you folks,'" Mom seethed as she told me that night.

"Your sister sat there taking it all in, but when she heard him say that, she sat up tall as could be, stared him right in the eye, and gave him the what-for." Now Mom was chuckling. Faced with the simple, straightforward reasoning of a ten-year-old, the man couldn't refuse.

"He was so shocked," said Mom, "that he agreed to help us right on the spot!"

Janie sat across from me, beaming and giggling. She was quite pleased with herself and didn't bother to hide it from us.

In the end, we didn't actually get any money from welfare, but my helper was on welfare herself, so somehow they set it up for her to work for me to get her subsistence pay. The welfare man had killed two birds with one stone, so to speak.

But my main care came down to Mom. Her job didn't pay much, it was long hours, and at night when she got home, she had the whole nurse routine to do again. Only this time it took longer because she had to cook dinner for us, do more chores, and get me into the tub for my nightly bath. She got me to bed every night. She did my bowel program every four days. Imagine having to dole out laxatives, wait two hours, then hold the bedpan under your grown son's ass, waiting for the laxative's results. Then clean him up like a helpless baby. That was the kind of stuff she had to do for me because the home health care woman didn't know how or would refuse to do a lot of things too.

Yet, Mom pushed through each day, just doing what was in front of her, never complaining. I didn't ever see her cry, but I know she did.

CLASS OF '67

The ultimate measure of a man is not where he stands in moments of comfort and convenience, but where he stands at times of challenge and controversy.

— Martin Luther King

During the Christmas break from school, Dr. Reed released me from Goettche Center. Mom and Gordy moved me home with bedpans, catheters, and surfboard in tow. Mom had already registered me at the Cody High School and I was scheduled to start the third quarter of my senior year back at my old stomping grounds. Gordy had taken the intercom speaker box with its hookups to my homeroom teacher, Mrs. Dunne. Between the two of them, they lined up some classmates of mine to haul the intercom box around from one classroom to the next. Mom got my class assignments and books and she showed the teachers how the speaker box worked.

Even though I was already used to using the speaker box in Thermopolis, I knew the kids in my classes, I recognized their voices, and I had a system with the teachers for me to ask questions during class. But now, back at Cody High, I didn't know my teachers or who was in my classes.

The first period of the first morning was English with Miss List—she sounded really nice on the speaker, and introduced me to the class.

"We have a new student today," she said. "You won't find him here in our classroom, though. He's joining us from his home by using this speaker box on my desk. Everyone, please welcome Will Alves to our class."

A jumble of voices echoed into my speaker, but one voice stood out: Christine's. My temple throbbed and I broke into a sweat. *Why didn't I think about this?* Of course, I'd probably run across Christine, and now it dawned on me that I'd see Vincent again too. I was so caught up in my anxiety that I almost missed my cue from the teacher.

"Will, we're so happy to have you back here at Cody again. Why don't you tell us a little about what you were reading in English when you left Hot Springs High?" Miss List was trying to break the ice, knowing everyone would be jumpy about my circumstances and coming back to my hometown school.

"We—we were reading *The Grapes of Wrath* by John Steinbeck."

"We haven't read that yet. Can you tell us a little bit

about the story?" Miss List nearly shouted into the loud-speaker, making me flinch.

"Well, it's about a family in the dust bowl of Oklahoma during the Depression, and they end up moving out to California to try to start over," I said.

The teacher took this as her chance to run with it and told us how Steinbeck won the Pulitzer Prize after the book was published in 1939. She raved about the merits of Steinbeck's story. My brain couldn't focus on her speech. I was too worried about what to say to Christine if she talked to me through the speaker box. Through the haze of my jittery mind, I heard only snippets of sentences...*an America divided into "haves" and "have-nots"... intense human drama...tragic but stirring.*

As Miss List droned on about injustice and the horrors of the Great Depression, I fell into a depression of my own. How was I going to face my best friend and my girlfriend, neither of whom I'd seen for over six months? The only time I'd seen Christine after the wreck was when I was still in the hospital at Billings. She and her dad had driven up to see me several weeks after the accident. Christine called my mom to see if it was okay, and Mom warned her to wait awhile because the swelling and bruises were still pretty awful - she'd watched people walking by my hospital room - they would gasp and look away, quickening their pace past my door.

When Christine and her dad came to visit, I was still on the rotating disk and still had the tongs sticking out

of my head. But my eyes weren't swollen, and the bruises had receded to a jaundiced yellow. Seeing Christine
started an avalanche in me: guilt over being with Rhonda
the night of the accident and knowing that Christine
knew; relief at seeing Christine again, especially when
she hugged me and gave me a kiss right on the lips; the
pain of realization that I couldn't hug her back; hope
with the flicker of our past passion for each other.

Christine wrote a few letters once I was settled in the
rehab center in Thermopolis, but those fizzled out after a
few months. I speculated who had moved in on my girl,
who was kissing her at night after the dances, who was
sitting with her in the swing on her porch. I came to the
conclusion it was most likely Quinn MacDonald. That
dog. He'd always had the hots for Christine. I'd deck the
bastard even if I had to throw a punch from this damn
chair.

Another visitor had showed up unannounced. Floyd
had convinced Vincent to come see me so he would know
I was going to be all right and hoping that we could make
peace with each other. They'd driven up from Cody on a
Friday night; it was late, well past visiting hours. I had no
idea how they'd sneaked in past the night charge nurse.
She had eagle eyes behind big-framed glasses, and the
sonar of a bat when it came to sensing rule breakers.

I'd been dozing off in bed, when I felt a presence
hovering at the door to my room. I opened my eyes
to two bulky shadows outlined by the hallway light. I

recognized Floyd's cowboy hat, and then gasped when I realized it was Vincent next to him. Floyd practically had to lead him over to my bed.

"Hey, Floyd. Hey, Vincent" was all I could muster.

"Hey, Will." Vincent tilted his head up until our eyes met. In the zero-sum of that moment, the blip of my surprise at seeing him gave way to my wretchedness. *Why wasn't it Vincent? Why did he get to walk away and I didn't?*

The adrenaline was pumping now, and sweat beaded on my forehead; the heat of my flushed skin spread to my neck. I was bent on picking a fight with him. *You ought to burn in hell for what you did to me!* I was yelling inside, and my face showed it all. He could read my thoughts and in the next instant, Vincent melted into the sterile linoleum, recoiling from me, shrinking back toward the door.

"Hey, sorry, man. I—I just don't even feel *human* half the time these days." He reeled as if to turn and run. "I have these nightmares, I can't sleep, can't eat without feeling like I'm going to barf."

Fear of him walking out drained my anger. "Please, Vincent, don't leave."

He stopped in the doorway, tears welling up.

"Please stay." My voice cracked, tears streaming down my face. "I need to talk to somebody that understands where I'm coming from. You're my best friend, man. You're the one that knows me better than anyone."

Vincent ran his hand through his hair, shrugged in that twitchy way he had.

Floyd, who'd been watching from the shadows, gently pushed a chair toward Vincent. He pulled it over to the bed and sat down.

"Will, you don't know the half of it. I need to tell you what's happening with me too."

He reached for my hand and wrapped my fingers around his in that grasp that we reserved only for the two of us. That's when I noticed the bruises on his arm and his neck, and the remnants of a shiner around his left eye.

He saw the alarm in my face.

"Well, I'm actually doing pretty good compared to what I looked like a month ago," he said, avoiding my eyes. "My old man, he beat the shit out of me when he found out about the accident."

"What?!" It was just like the bastard, same as Leon— always beating on us to turn us into *real men*. "As if you didn't feel bad enough already, huh?!"

"Yeah," Vincent said, staring at the floor. "He—he told me I have to stay away from you. I'm taking a big chance just being here tonight."

"Why? That's crazy! We're best friends!" This was unbelievable.

"Well, you might not know this yet, I'm not sure. But your insurance company is suing me and my family for the accident. My dad said we're going to lose everything—our house, our land, the cattle—everything."

"Holy shit! I had no idea about this," I said. "Mom

hasn't mentioned a thing to me."

"It's all confusing to me, but somehow the insurance people bypassed a jury trial and went to the state court asking for a judgment against me."

"You're not to blame, Vincent. It wasn't your fault. It wasn't anyone's fault. It just happened."

"I tell myself that, but I don't believe it, not really. After the beating and the screaming at first, now Dad doesn't even look at me, doesn't say a word to me. It's worse than the bruises and black eye. I'm leaving as soon as I can and enlisting early if they'll take me."

"Jesus H. Christ, Vincent! I don't know what to say, man. And I don't know if I can get through this without you."

We talked into the early morning, trying to make sense of the whole thing, wondering what we could do to preserve our bond with each other. We didn't have any answers when he left, and I never saw Vincent again.

WILL: GRADUATION DAY

Our greatest glory consists not in never falling,
but in rising every time we fall.

— Oliver Goldsmith

I'd struggled through months of classes and mounds of homework, trying not to fall behind. I had to keep my grades up so I wouldn't have to re-do my senior year. The frantic schedule kept me from feeling sorry for myself. Now it was Graduation Day—May 28, 1967.

It was with a fair amount of dread that I faced the day. This would be the first summer that I wouldn't go back to the Hudson Ranch. I'd spent every summer there since I was twelve. While I was getting dressed that morning for the graduation ceremonies, my mind drifted back to the last time I was there.

It was the summer of '64. I tried working in Cody with Leon, Stepfather Number Three, when school got out. Leon helped get me hired on at the X-L Ranch on Jim Mountain Road. We'd drive out there together and stay the week unless the weather shut things down. Then we'd get the night off to come into town to have supper with Mom, Gordy, and Janie.

I liked Mom's cooking most of the time, but Gordy and I teased her anyway.

"Boys, do you remember that sausage and lima bean casserole I made a while back? You know, the one I called my 'Sunday Surprise'?"

"Yeah, Mom. We called it our 'Monday Surprise.'" I jabbed Gordy's arm and he took the hint.

"And it became my 'Tuesday Surprise.'" Gordy jabbed me back; we chuckled over our joke.

But Leon came unglued.

"Don't you boys EVER be that disrespectful to your mother again!" He grabbed both of us around our necks and slammed our heads together. "Any more bullshit like that, and I'll take my belt to you."

He didn't know how to take a joke, or maybe he just wanted to throw his weight around with us, to show us who's boss. He was just plain mean and cruel. I hated the bastard.

One morning, driving back out to South Fork, Leon confronted me again. "You know, I didn't realize that cars could *make* gas. The tank is fuller than it was last night. And this windshield was sure dirty when we came to town. But it's nice and clean this morning!" We worked all day without another word between the two of us.

Next day, he pestered me again.

"How do you suppose that gas tank registered so full, and how did the car windows get so clean just being parked on the street all night?"

I knew if I didn't confess, if I kept it to myself, I'd get a "lesson" that I'd "never forget" just like the dozens of times before when he came home drunk, looking for a fight.

"The car wasn't parked out front all night. I took the car and made Gordy come with me. We sneaked out the bedroom window and jumped off the porch roof after you and Mom went to bed."

"And just how did you happen to have the keys?" Red eyes flared in his swarthy face, just a few inches from me.

"I—I made a copy of the key a few weeks ago when Mom sent me to the grocery store." Mom didn't have a clue; she never checked the mileage or the gas gauge. But Leon was smart about those things; he was always suspicious of us, even when we tried to be good and honest. Mom thought that Leon was a good influence on us boys, that he made us "toe the mark."

But the beatings came more often, and the bruises went deep; it was more than just a sore jaw or bloody nose. It was about control and oppression. I was big and I was strong, but I was still a kid. I wanted to believe in him. I wanted all those ups and downs that fathers and sons have. I never trusted him; never knew when I'd set off the next explosion in him. I couldn't stand being around him anymore.

I called Lawrence Hudson and asked if he still needed a hand for the summer at his Colorado ranch. By the first of July, I was on my way to Walden. It was my fourth summer working for Lawrence, and I was glad to be going back.

We'd moved there when I was twelve. At first, I was mad about leaving my friends and starting over in a strange town. I found out right away the kids I met in Walden were just like my buddies back home. Nothing to worry about, really. I started playing basketball. The other guys liked having me on the team because I was tall and could shoot three-pointers pretty well.

At sixteen, I looked and felt much different than the twelve-year-old kid I used to be. My buddies had changed too—we were all cocky and general smart-asses. Every Saturday night, I'd ask Mr. Hudson for my week's pay and head out to party all night. He put up with me for about three weeks. On a Sunday morning, he caught up with me in the milk separating room.

"Will, the partying has to stop now or you can go look for another job."

I knew there weren't many other job prospects around that small Colorado town. I couldn't go back to Cody before summer was over—I had to earn my school money or Mom and Leon would have a fit. I looked at Lawrence and realized my respect for this man overpowered my desire to whoop it up in town with the boys.

"Okay, sir. You're right—I need to find something else to do with my free time."

I found entertainment in an old .410 shotgun and lots of shells. I'd take the tractor out to the prairie dog grounds and shoot the hell out of them in the evenings. I'd even go out on days we got rained out of the hay fields.

A few weeks later, I found a pair of sixteen-ounce boxing gloves stuffed into the corner of the barn. Lawrence had hired a Mexican boy as hay hand that summer, and he wanted to learn how to box. We'd go at it for hours at a time, me showing him the boxing moves that Leon had passed on to me.

With his son Rafe in England for the summer, Lawrence was running the hay crew by himself. He was beginning to trust me again, seeing that I'd made a turn-around and wasn't partying and boozing it up.

"Will, I want you to take charge of the hay stacking crew. The rain's put us behind and I need to be doing some other chores while you boys are out haying."

"Thanks, Mr. Hudson! I know I can handle it—I won't let you down," I said, grateful for his confidence in me. I felt like I was maturing and becoming a man that day.

It was getting close to Labor Day weekend and we still had a lot of hay to cut, bale, and stack. I decided to call in reinforcements. That evening after supper, I dialed up my best friend, Rex Walker.

"Rex, I need you here at Hudson's. I've got to be back

in Cody in ten days for school, and we've got a shitload of hay to put up. Can you make it?" I called Carl Tucker too, and he said he could come help us on the weekend.

Rex drove out that Sunday and worked with us all week. On the last day, I broke my knuckle on my little finger, but I wore my work glove over the swollen hand so I could still stack hay.

We'd finished all the hay needed for the year. We went into town to celebrate before going our separate ways. We'd just pulled into the parking lot around eight when a rusty pickup lurched in beside us, doors flying open before coming to a stop. Three cowboys scuttled into the bar.

"They're just looking for some easy chicks," I told Rex. "Like them." I pointed to four well-known girls rounding the corner of the building.

"Yeah, it'll be a high time in the old Stockman tonight!" Rex switched on the radio. He found our favorite station and tuned it to Chubby Checker singing "The Twist." Carl reached under the seat and pulled out a fifth of Calvert's.

I grabbed the Coke bottles from the backseat and popped the tops with Ferdinand.

"You still use that crazy thing to open your bottles?" asked Rex.

"Yeah, it's a conversation piece with the chicks, and besides, it still works great!" I held the miniature silver bull up for inspection—the horns formed the bottle opener at one end, and the tail was a corkscrew.

We swigged our Cokes down until we could add some whiskey and watched more people as they filed into the bar. We'd just polished off our drinks and stepped out of the car when we heard someone hollering around the side of the building.

"Sounds like a fight!" Rex took off running; Carl and I were close behind. Two guys were wallowing in the gravel, groping at clothes and arms, fists jabbing at each other's faces. The four girls, two of the cowboys, and some city boy stood watching and cheering on their favorite fighter.

As my eyes adjusted to the shadow cast by the building, I recognized one of the brawlers—Murdock, the third cowboy. An unfamiliar face stared up at him as he flung himself on top and punched him in the side. I pushed the girls aside, grabbed Murdock under the shoulders, and stood him up.

"Leave him alone, Murdock!"

He jerked loose and whipped around to face me. "Nobody ever hauls *me* out of a fight, fatso!"

"I don't *start* fights like you do, asshole, so let's even this up, one on one, you and me."

"Screw you, man." Murdock wrenched away from me and grabbed one of the girls' arms. "Let's go to my pickup for a beer."

"Thanks," said the city boy. His pants muddy and torn, he turned and wobbled toward the bar, leaning on his friend's arm.

"No problem. I don't like trouble. What's more, I don't like troublemakers like Murdock," I replied.

We all walked in at the same time, the city boys sliding into a booth near the door while Rex, Carl, and I found spaces at the bar. We stood using the foot railing, ordering our drinks.

"Will, you snagged Murdock off that guy like he was a feather! That Golden Gloves training beefed you up quite a bit," Rex said.

I puffed my chest a little more when I heard his admiration.

"Yeah, old Leon wasn't good for much, but he sure did teach me to box," I replied. Stepfather Number Three was a brawling cowboy who had taken the District Heavyweight Championship and held it for four years. I was following in his footsteps in that regard, and scheduled to go to District in the spring. "I'd just as soon have all my fights in the ring instead of the parking lot or alley. But I have a rep that marks me. Once you get a reputation, any hotshot who thinks he can scrap always wants to take you on."

"I wouldn't worry about that much," Carl said as he surveyed the smoky saloon. I read his mind.

"Do you suppose Kay and Linda will be in soon, or should we see if we can go find 'em?"

A hazy beacon from the street lamp lit up the dance hall for a moment as the door swung open. We looked toward the door, but instead of the girls, there was Murdock, staggering in with his date.

"Ignore him." Rex was reading my mind now. "The bartender will get rid of him in short order."

I turned back to the bar when I heard a gruff, "Hey, fat boy," to my right. "Let me through. I need a drink."

I saw the bastard in the mirror's reflection behind the bar—his sunken cheeks and lumpy nose, the scar on his chin, the ratty hair. He didn't deserve an answer.

"You gonna move, tubby?" he said sharply. "Or am I gonna have to move ya?"

I could hear his buddies trying to coax him to the back table. "Come on, Murdock. Don't start something in here." "Pass it up, Murdock." "Let's just have another beer and forget this loser."

Yeah, go have another beer. You really don't want to deal with me again tonight, asshole.

"No! This lard-ass is blocking my way!"

I could feel the crowd gathering behind us, trying to catch the words and gauging my reaction. I just stared at him through the mirror on the back bar.

"There's plenty of room to go around," said Carl.

Murdock grabbed my shoulder and swung my body around. I slammed my left fist under his rib cage, then delivered the right cross to his jaw. He heaved backward, plunging into his friends.

A flash of disbelief crossed their faces as Murdock regained his balance. "I'll tear you apart, you moosey

SOB," yelled Murdock, shaking his arms loose from his friends' grips.

By then, Al the bartender had pushed through the crowd and stood between us. "Take it outside, boys," he rasped. "Or do I need to call the cops?"

"I don't fight drunks." I looked Murdock in the eye for an instant, then turned back as if to make a comment to Rex.

"You're scared as hell," he sneered back. "You know I can kick the shit out of you, huh?"

"Afraid not, Murdock." I grinned. "I just don't want to interrupt this party."

"The 'party' would be on me." He laughed.

"Get out of here, Murdock," Al roared.

Murdock laughed louder and Al shoved him toward the door. "I think the real chickenshit is coming through now!"

"Don't go out there for a while, Will," Al warned me. "They're probably waiting for you."

"We're in no hurry," replied Carl and Rex, who'd been glued to my side the whole time.

The speakers blared out "Little Deuce Coupe" just as Kay and Linda strolled in and made a beeline for us. We forgot all about Murdock for the rest of the night.

♠ ♣ ♥ ♦

Mom's voice jerked me back. "Will, hurry up! We need to get you down to the school—graduation starts at one and it's already noon!"

I saw my image in the mirror. My gnarled hand held the hairbrush, poised for a last-minute adjustment. Desperate thoughts crashed into my mind. Hands that would never lift another bale of hay. Arms that would never hold a girl again. No more boxing. No wrestling tournaments. If I wasn't going back to the ranch, what was I going to do? What *could* I do now, with this broken body? Christ, how was I even going to get through this day?

WILL: SURFING

Smooth seas do not make skillful sailors.

— African Proverb

"You have a very bright future, Will," said Mr. Tsosie. "You have the whole world in front of you now."

"Yeah, right. Whatever you say." My case worker from the Wyoming Vocational Rehab Program was sitting at the dining room table with me.

"We can get you enrolled in the Billings Business College this summer. An accounting degree would suit you well." His choppy Northern Arapaho voice grated on me.

"Sure, why not?" What did I have to lose? I had nothing better to do. I was strapped to my surfboard when he showed up, lying face down over the back of the wheelchair. Even now, I still had to use the contraption from time to time when the damned bedsores flared up.

Mr. Tsosie shoved the papers under my nose, onto the table below me. Listless, I skimmed through the registration papers and class descriptions. *Accounting? You've got to be kidding.* All I had wanted to do after graduating was learn how to run those big road construction machines. That conversation with Mom seemed like an eternity ago now: going to school in Idaho to get my equipment operator's license. Bean counting was the furthest thing from my macho eighteen-year-old mind.

"Now that your court case is settled, you'll have the means to get set up there. We can help you arrange for home health care. Our agency can service clients in Montana *and* Wyoming."

Shortly after my accident, the lawyer took Mom to Red Lodge to see where it happened. Not long after that, Mr. Andrews and his partner got a court hearing in Cody to decide if the insurance company had to pay us. We'd asked for $75,000, I think, but I don't remember the exact amount. The attorneys ended up negotiating the settlement for around half that amount. We paid the attorneys their fees. The rest of the money would be used for my care and whatever else Mom and I decided I would need.

Mr. Tsosie knew we'd received a settlement. He wanted to spend our money. But, to his credit, he was also volunteering his program funds to make this happen.

So Gordy and I made plans to move to Billings. After getting my two-year degree, the goal was to come back to Cody, where I would run my own business. Supplying duplicating statement and billing systems, advertising and visual aids for small businesses. Whoopee.

We had to act fast. Summer session started June 5th and this was already the beginning of May. The wheels started turning, and before I knew it, we'd secured an apartment on Avenue C, got me enrolled in the college, and hired a home health care nurse.

I was even somewhat of a celebrity. *The Gazette* got wind of me and wrote an article: "Call Him Undaunted," the July 1967 headlines read. A photograph of me was splashed across the Sunday Magazine. A thick canvas strap adhered me to the surfboard, and my patterned pajama bottoms adorned my legs. I was lying face down over the back of the wheelchair and peeking at the camera like a one-eyed jack, anchoring my hand on the edge of the table. A glass with a straw sat nearby and an open textbook lay under me on the tabletop. There was a whole write-up about me and how I was an "example for anyone who thinks he is disabled" and thinks they are in better shape than me, as my caseworker, Tsosie, was quoted as saying. It was more a plug for how all these agencies were helping me more than the hurdles I had to clear to get where I was. Still, I was flattered that they did a story about me.

By the time I started school, we'd acquired a push-button telephone, a yellow '63 Corvair van for transport, hand braces and porta-lifts, the used hospital bed from Cody, and even a felt pen with a sponge taped to the end of it. The sponge-pen allowed me to type twenty-three words per minute with no errors. I discovered early on that changing books and flipping pages was more labor-intensive than the typing. I didn't care for business college, but it was something to do. Best of all, we had a party house for the summer.

Imagine me, the eighteen-year-old cripple and his fifteen-year-old brother, living on our own for an entire summer in the big city of Billings! What the newspaper article didn't disclose was our demented lifestyle that escalated as summer marched on.

I had a knack for looking older than I was, and the wheelchair was a great prop. Gordy would wheel me over to Buck's Bar, a few blocks away from the apartment. We'd go in and order our booze. Nobody ever asked me for ID, whether they were embarrassed about the wheelchair or what, I don't know. But I kept us supplied with liquor all summer.

The apartment building we lived in had eight units. Since it was summer, there was lots of activity outside. That's when we met Sherry's mom.

"Hi, boys! It looks like you're heading out early today."

"Yeah, Will has school starting at 8:30 and I'm his chauffeur." Gordy wheeled me aside so she could pass us on the sidewalk. "Have a good day, ma'am."

"Oh, don't call me 'ma'am'—I have a daughter about your age, so I'm not *that* old." She flashed a pleasant smile toward Gordy. "Why don't you boys stop by this evening if you're around at six? I'm in number three. I'll fix you some snacks. I'm Nancy Owens. And you are?"

"I'm Gordy and this is my big brother Will. Glad to meet you!"

Sherry picked my twisted hand up from the armrest of the wheelchair and shook it delicately. She looked right into my eyes and I stared back, mesmerized by those light blue orbs. For a mom, she was a real looker.

"Thanks, Mrs. Owens. We might just take you up on your offer."

She glided past us on three-inch heels, her blue skirt twirling around shapely legs.

That night after school, we'd just got back from our Buck's Bar run and wanted to check out her offer. Gordy wheeled me over to apartment three, knocked softly, and stood aside.

She answered the door, still in the flippy blue skirt and low-cut top. "Come on in, guys," she said as she swept the door open for us. She'd laid out tons of snacks, but even better, her daughter Sherry and her friend Kat were in the kitchen, giggling and setting out more delectable dishes for us.

Gordy was smitten with Kat at first glance. Petite with fiery green eyes and black hair, she had a quick laugh. Not a frilly laugh, but a good belly laugh. She was also sarcastic and funny at the same time. I could tell this was going to get interesting. For the rest of the summer, we spent a lot of time at Mrs. Owen's apartment, and she kept us well supplied with party people. Including Sherry and Kat. They were the same age, sixteen that summer. According to Gordy's report three weeks into it, Kat's mom had her on birth control pills, so it was *really* on for him.

While Gordy and Kat hit it off, I had a hard time with girls. I knew they wouldn't really be interested in me because I was paralyzed, and that made it even harder to approach a girl. It was easier for me to talk to Sherry's mom, Nancy. It took the pressure off me to look for a girlfriend. I sure missed having relationships with girls, though. I thought back to Cody — to Christine Kingsley. She'd come pick me up in her dad's car and we'd cruise around Cody all night. I thought I was pretty hot stuff riding in the sheriff's patrol car with my girl!

The summer continued, and more visitors showed up on our doorstep. Even though we spent a good amount of time with Kat and Sherry and her mom, most of the summer was a male bonding experience.

Once our buddies from Cody got wind that we were living in Billings in our own apartment, they showed up on the weekends by the carload. Mostly it was Floyd, Terry, and the Duval kid. They were my best friends and party pals when I lived in Cody.

I remember one time Tim Cole came up — he had that hot '61 Chevy. He and Gordy went out and burned around the point. Tim did a burnout right in front of the police station. Gordy said the cops were looking out the window at them. They took off fast and pulled it off the street between the apartments to keep it hidden. The last thing we needed was for them to get busted.

I kept up on my studying despite our antics on the weekends. I didn't miss any school. I had a couple of cures for hangovers. Like sticking my fingers down my throat and emptying my stomach out before going to sleep. And a couple of Alka-Seltzers and aspirins before going to sleep. But once I had those contorted hands, I couldn't do the retching. I'd just have Gordy fix the "plop-plop-fizz-fizz" and call it good. I discovered that I liked mixed drinks more than beer — beer filled my leg bag up too much, a cause of embarrassment when the girls were around.

One morning we got up late for school. Gordy rushed around, getting breakfast for me and loading me up in the Corvair. It had a side door, and he'd just tip the wheelchair back on the rear wheels and lift me into the back of the van, strapping the wheels down once he got me situated. There weren't any windows in the back of the van, so it was dark and dingy for most transports. He got me to school on time. But neither one of us noticed that something was missing. Until I was rolling down the hallway to class.

"You forgot my leg bag, you bastard!" I yelled at him through the pay phone in the school's lobby. "I'm all backed up and need to pee, and I mean *now*!"

Gordy rushed back and picked me up, hauled me back home so he could get me fixed up.

Floyd was a regular on the weekends. He really was my best friend through all of the shit, and he knew that Vincent couldn't be there for me. Anyway, we'd been partying a lot that night, and Gordy was really out of it. First we got neighbor Nancy to walk him around the block a few times to try to sober him up. While they were walking around, this car pulled up with four hoods in it. They gave Gordy a bad time and he ended up fighting all four of them. When he showed up at the apartment, all beat to hell, Floyd took him over to the car wash and literally hosed Gordy down to sober him up. Then they went looking for those hoods, but they never found them that night.

Another regular visitor was Mr. Tsosie. He'd call to say he was flying up to check on us, which he had to do to make his report to Voc Rehab in order to keep the money coming in for my care and the rent. Most of the time, we knew he was coming, so Gordy would rush around and clean the place up, throw out the empty beer cans and such; you know, spruce up the place. Then he'd go pick Tsosie up at the airport. He'd crash on our couch for the night and snore so loud even the neighbors complained they couldn't sleep. One time, Tsosie didn't phone ahead. He wanted to see what we were up to without knowing he was around.

Gordy and I had made our usual rounds, wheeling

to the grocery store and then Buck's for supplies. We'd already left the grocery store when we discovered we hadn't paid for the watermelon—it was sitting in my lap! Gordy didn't notice it there and I couldn't feel it sitting on my legs, so neither one of us thought of it. We were joking around about it in Buck's when we heard someone laughing too, back in the corner. We couldn't see who it was and just shrugged it off. Turns out it was Tsosie, watching us buy booze. He was a stand-up man, though, and didn't bust us or cut off our money—nothing like that.

I think they were ready to expel me from business school by summer's end. But by then, Mom had decided to move to Billings. She felt that, to afford the resources for my care and education, we needed to live here. She knew that I wouldn't get those things in a small town like Cody. So, I quit school, promising her that I'd look into getting into something else. But I was also pissed about the whole thing. We had to give up our apartment to go live with Mom and my little sister. Party time was over.

WILL: BABY SISTER

Hippies? Why, I'm the original

— Jerry Lee Lewis

My college days were full, but my nights were even fuller. I was there most evenings when my little sister Janie would get home from junior high school, loaded with homework and stories about her day. We spent hours together at the dining room table, pouring over our books and talking.

"What do you have for homework tonight?" This was my daily question to her.

"The usual. You know, history, English, algebra. Hey did you know that algebra was invented by an Arab guy? Yeah, Mohammed something. He was a mathematician and he wrote a book called 'al-jabr' and that's how we got the word algebra!"

"You don't say? Well, why don't we take a look at

that Al Jabber stuff and see if we can hammer it out?"

"I guess so." Rolling of the eyes.

She'd open the book and prop it up on my reading stand that held the pages open for me to read. We'd sit there, each of us doing our homework, talking and joking about the day's events. The house rule was, she had to finish her homework first and then start cooking dinner, which amounted to just opening a few cans of vegetables and heating them on the stove, along with leftovers that Mom had carefully packaged and left in the fridge. She'd set the table and when Mom got home, we'd eat dinner together. It wasn't Beaver Cleaver's family, but it was comfortable for us.

Sometimes Gordy wouldn't have to work at the gas station, and he'd join us, too. Most nights, though, he was either working or hanging out across town with Kat at her place. He was a senior and nearly an adult, she said. I think she just had so much on her plate that she was too tired to enforce the house rules with him.

All those after-school nights forged a special bond with me and my little sister. We spent many hours together, and I lived vicariously through her and her many adventures as a teen-ager. There were times when I could see trouble brewing, though, and I had to step in and put the skids to her hair-brained schemes.

Like the time she came home from the outdoor concert at Pioneer Park. She'd spent all of a Sunday there with her friends, mostly innocent stuff like listening to the local punks play their dismal imitations of the Stones, Grand Funk Railroad, and the like. But, when she got home, I knew something was not right. She was high on drugs, I was sure of that.

"So…what bands played today?"

"I can't remember the band names! The Band Aids? Hee, hee!"

"What's so funny about that? Come here, let me smell your breath."

"Geez, what's your problem? I haven't been smoking pot, if that's what you mean."

"It that's true, then you won't mind letting me take a whiff of your breath."

When she got close enough to me, I could tell her eyes were dilated, black orbs where the brown should be. She leered closer than usual to me, staring into my eyes with a Cheshire grin.

"What're you on? You're higher than a kite!"

"You're full of bullshit, you know that? I'm going to my room."

She knew that *I* knew the gig was up and that I always knew when she was high. As soon as she'd walk in, I'd try to roll my chair over to her. But, she'd rush for the stairs and fling the door open, disappearing into the black hole of the basement. How I wish I could use my damn legs again and go down there after her. I was terrified she'd end up on some street corner, pushing drugs for some scrawny, asshole pimp, or found dead in the alley with tracks on her arms. I'd sit there in my chair, listening to the bass booming on her stereo below me, trembling with rage and sweating in fear.

The fear drove me to take over the father role, the disciplinarian, the guardian. I couldn't stand to see her do those things. But, she always did her homework and chores, and she always got good grades. She didn't skip school and she really liked her teachers. I could see that she was a good girl. She just had some shady influences. Kind of like me in my early days at Walden and Cody. I didn't want her to take the same path. What could I do - a cripple in a wheelchair - that would make a difference to her?

I could tie up her time, for one thing. I suggested she get a part-time job so she could have spending money, especially since Mom didn't have money to give her in the first place.

We started looking in the want ads, and I coached her on what to say when she called about jobs. We'd fill out the applications together. If she had to apply in person, she'd "model" her clothes for me to see if they passed the test.

"How's this? This leather mini-skirt with the fringe and the halter top is coolest outfit I have."

"It *is* cool. But how about just this time, you wear those cute bell bottoms that Mom made you and wear your white shirt with them? Those are every bit as cool as this outfit."

She took my advice and I just about fell out of my chair when she landed a job. At age fifteen, Janie was one of the first gingham-checked waitresses at the new Country Kitchen on Grand Avenue. We celebrated that night with vanilla ice cream and chocolate syrup. Lots of syrup. She had to work most every night, even weekends, so I knew then that I'd scored a major coup in keeping her out of trouble.

We hung out together on weekends, too. I bribed her into cribbage contests, or played Yahtzee, and a lot of Sundays were spent at our aunt and uncle's house on Park Hill. They'd moved to Billings almost the same time we did, and it was great spending lazy Sunday afternoons with them, eating a big dinner and playing cards.

Those were the times I felt the most normal. Nobody stared at my gnarled hands or my chrome steed. Nobody cared if I had to ask Mom to empty my leg bag. We told jokes and family stories and laughed a lot. Uncle Richard was a comedian in my books. He was one of my heroes. He was good to Janie, too. I was glad to have an ally to help with her teen-age ways. If she and our cousin Alan were outside throwing the football or climbing trees, sometimes Uncle Richard and I would consult about how to handle these unruly teens. He was full of good advice, stuff I could really use.

I was also taking upper coursework classes in Psychology at college. By this time in the game, I'd decided that I wasn't going to be a business man. I was fascinated by human behavior, so I'd switched my major to Psych. I loved trying out the things I learned on my little sister, to see what really worked and what didn't. I even wrote a bunch of papers on it. After awhile, she got wise to my "experiments" and found ways to sabotage being the guinea pig. It became a contest to see who could outwit who. Most of the time, I won. She was good-natured about it, though.

Janie had always been agreeable and naïve. I remembered times at the yellow duplex in Cody, before my accident, when Gordy and I would want to go downtown and chase girls. We didn't want Janie tagging along, so we'd get her to play "Houdini." We'd tell her we'd give her a giant-size Butterfinger if she could escape the athletic sock bondage routine.

"Yeah, it really was one of Houdini's tricks!" We'd tell her as we tied her up to the banister on the stairs, figuring we'd have a good hour before we had to be back at the house. She got really good at escaping, though, and sometimes we'd have to high tail it back in thirty minutes or less. She'd be waiting for us, tinkering with her Barbie dolls, jubilant in her glory and bragging about how easy it was to foil us.

As fun as it was to match wits with my little sister, my main goal evolved into a desire to be a counselor for other disabled people, guys like me that were stuck in a wheelchair. I knew I could help others find a sense of independence and self-esteem. I could motivate them to keep going no matter what the odds. Been there, done that. I could show them the way to success as a paralyzed person whose life had changed so dramatically. I'd started out as a seventeen-year-old boy dreaming of riding road graders and moving tons of dirt to doing the mental spade work it takes to get into someone's mind and find out what makes them tick, to help other poor bastards like me design a new plan for living.

WILL: NURSES - TAKE TWO

Always drink upstream from the herd.

— Will Rogers

Mom was exhausted with working and doing all of my daily care, so once we got things settled with the agency to get an aide to come in, we put an ad in the paper. That's when I met Russell.

"Hello. This is Russell Roy. I'm calling about your ad for the home health aide," he boomed through the receiver in his cowboy drawl.

What kind of man could he be? With a name like Russell Roy and sounding like a rough, tough ranch hand?

"Sure," I said. "You saw in the ad that I'm quadriplegic, so tell me about your experience with helping disabled people."

"I took care of my uncle for a couple of years after he was paralyzed from a stroke, and filled in as relief nurse at the Roundup Hospital while I was living with my aunt and uncle."

"Why are you applying for this job with me?"

"I'm looking to find work in Billings now. My uncle's in a nursing home, and there's not much to do up here in Roundup."

We talked more about his know-how when it came to avoiding pressure sores and exercising my arms and legs for range of motion and strength. He'd managed his uncle's bowel and bladder programs too, which was a big deal when it came to my care.

We set up a meeting for a couple of days later. When he showed up at the door, he confirmed my impression of him. He didn't fit the stereotype profile of a male nurse. His tall, lanky frame barely fit as he stepped through the door. He swept his Stetson off his handsome head to greet my mom.

"How do you do, Mrs. Alves?" He held her hand gently in his and I swear she almost giggled like a schoolgirl. He walked over to me, wrapped my fingers around his hand, and gave me a firm shake. This guy knew about being paralyzed all right. "It's a pleasure to meet you, Will."

We spent the afternoon shooting the breeze. When he found out what a practical joker I was, he told some stories about his stint at the hospital.

"I'm a wiseacre too." Russell said he'd tease the nurses on the floor. "Yeah, I'd tell them to find me when they needed a lift, or 'make sure to let me know when you need a Y-chromosome opinion about those shoes you're wearing.'"

I felt at ease with Russell. He was likeable and we had a lot in common — we were both practical jokers. We swapped a few more pleasantries, and then I got down to brass tacks.

"Russell, I need to let you know what the attendant's duties are and what I expect. I've typed up a list here, so take a look at this and then we can talk about any questions you might have."

I handed him the packet: eight pages of instructions and three more pages of job description.

"Jesus H. Christmas," he blurted. "I wasn't expecting to read a novel."

"Sure, buddy. I know it's a pain, but I want to make sure there are no surprises for either of us, if I do decide to hire you. Go ahead, take your time reading this. I'm sure you'll have a few questions too."

He took the papers from me. The first one began:

A.M. ROUTINE

1. *By the time you arrive (no later than 7:00 a.m.), I will have had my morning medications and my breakfast, so you will need to start my bathwater and make it fairly warm to hot. While the water is running in the tub, cut ten pieces of tape (six are five inches long, two are six inches long, and two more that are two inches long) and*

put them on the sponges.

2. *If it is catheter change day, open a catheter packet and keep it ready by the bed.*

3. *Turn bathwater off when it's one-half inch below the overflow drain.*

4. *Put the bath sling under me with the end that the two holes are closest toward the head. Remember to bend my legs way up at the knees when turning me. Attach the sling by hooking the grommets to the lift. Jack the lift up and roll me into the bathroom to the tub. Pin the lift to the tub. THIS IS VERY IMPORTANT!!! You have to get the legs of the lift all the way up against the sink cabinet in order to get the pin to slide all the way into lock position.*

Russell was a slow reader but a quick study. He commented about a lot of the instructions, letting me know that he had either done those pieces before, or asking questions about the things he was unfamiliar with. I could tell he was nervous, and he joked about some of my terminology, like "dillies" and "egg crate."

He told me about his work experience. He expanded on his comments from our phone call, especially his work at the rural hospital. After that, he fell quiet and fidgeted a bit in his chair. I decided to change the subject and give him a chance to relax.

I asked him, "What was it like at the hospital, working with so many good-looking women?"

"You've never seen the nurses at Roundup, have you? There weren't that many that were young and pretty like me."

"Ha-ha," I said with a grin.

He said, "It had its ups and downs. The downside was that I'd get blamed every time when things went awry, but the upside was the overflow from the uniform tops. I had to play a running loop in my head. 'Don't look at the boobs. Don't look at the boobs. Don't look at the boobs.' But I looked anyway."

It didn't take him long to unwind. He went on:

"Don't ask the nurses if they're having a bad hair day. They start asking the questions—the endless questions. Does it always look bad to you? Is it too short? Too long? Should I pull it up? Should I leave it down? And don't EVER ask them if it's 'that time of the month' because you'll get a new butt hole ripped for that one!"

He was a crack-up, but he knew about the medical stuff too. He could help me set up my medical schedule for dispensing my prescriptions. He could check vital signs and know when things were going south.

Russell came to work for me a few weeks later. He was a damn good nurse. Russell was a lifesaver when it came to my hygiene program. It had been downright embarrassing to have my mom wash my privates and take care of my bowel program. Even though I'd never dreamed it would be another male handling my family jewels—I always dreamed about my wife doing that—it was easier to take than having my mother doing these things.

More than just being my caregiver, he was my right-hand man — someone I could count on, to shoot the bull with, or just to hang out with. I'd left friends behind in Cody and had to start all over in Billings. Being home-bound didn't help. I met a few fellows when I started college, but hardly anyone had the inclination to hang out with a guy in a wheelchair. They were too busy playing sports or chasing girls. I could understand that. It was what I really wanted to do too. Russell took the sting out of my isolation and loneliness. He'd stick around after doing my morning routine and have a cup of coffee, or he'd load me up in his '53 International Harvester pick-up truck and we'd run around doing errands.

Russell knew about honor and shame. He gave me back my dignity, and it wasn't until he came along that I was able to move on, and not merely subsisting but really starting to live again.

Then, once again, I was destined to have a friendship cut short.

Russell had been living in an old rundown farmhouse in Boyd and driving in every day for my care. He had some pasture land there, enough to run a handful of horses. He was always wheeling and dealing with ranchers, trading horses with them or buying them and then taking them to Lewistown to sell at the public auctions.

It was interesting how he'd come across some of

these animals and how he tried so hard to make money from his "side business." One of his acquaintances, Mrs. Patterson, got him involved with a crazy situation. She knew that Russell owned several horses and had the land to house them, so she called to tell him that a mare had wandered onto her land; she wanted him to come over to have a look.

She'd told Russell, "I don't know who the horse belongs to; I left it alone for a while, thinking the owner would come by and pick her up, but no one has showed up."

"Is this your horse, Russell?" she asked when he showed up at her place.

"No, ma'am, it isn't mine," he said.

According to Mrs. Patterson, when she later testified in court, the mare had disappeared several days after the visit from Russell. Livestock inspectors from Billings and Lewistown (where an auction took place in February) testified that Russell had brought the mare and two other horses in to try to sell. A well-hidden tattoo on the inside lower lip of one was the clincher — the evidence came straight from the horse's mouth, as they say. The judge handed down the maximum sentence — a horse thief in Montana earns a felony conviction of ten years. Russell went to prison, and I went on the hunt for a new home care attendant.

BEVERLY: HEARTS

*Life is not a matter of holding good cards,
but sometimes, playing a poor hand well.*

— Jack London

Life started to feel normal again at one point. I'd been working at the doctors' offices for quite some time. Will had been taking college classes, and he seemed to like the direction he'd taken with the psychology courses. Gordy, already married to Kat and with a small baby to boot, was out on his own. And little Janie was humming right along in high school, getting good grades and working as a waitress after school.

My cousin Velda and her family had moved to Billings too, which thrilled me. I felt like I could have some sort of social outlet with them. They also helped us establish a feeling of being a family again. More times than not, we'd spend Sunday afternoons at their house having dinner and playing cards. When we arrived in the afternoon, the men hauled Will up the steps in his wheelchair. They'd also put wooden blocks under the dining table and shore up the dining table legs so Will could roll his wheelchair underneath the tabletop and join in the fun.

We had a lovely meal, as always. Velda had prepared a chuck roast with mashed potatoes and green beans. I brought my homemade dinner rolls and an apple pie. There was ice cream for the pie and coffee to go with it.

We always played cards afterward. We'd swing from pinochle to hearts to gin rummy. If the others petered out, a few of us would play cribbage. We had running bets from week to week as to who would be the grand winner.

I felt like I could breathe again. After those first few years of struggling, not wanting to accept the fact that our lives had turned upside down, we gained an acceptance and a sort of contentment about where we were and how far we'd come.

Today, we decide to play hearts, since there are an odd number of us wanting to play. We use a double deck, and Richard deals the first hand. Everyone gets thirteen cards. I've brought Will's wooden card holder, a long rectangle with a groove in it for standing the cards up. He can barely get all those cards lined up! Gordy had made it in shop class at school with the idea of us playing cribbage, which doesn't require as many cards for a hand.

On the first hand, once everyone is dealt their thirteen cards, we pass three cards face-down to the person on our left. Then we start playing, with both the cards we were dealt and the three passed to us. Usually, there are a lot of groans when people pick up their three cards from their neighbor!

I have the two of clubs, so I lead the hand. The play goes clockwise from me, with everyone playing clubs if they have them, and if not, they can play another suit. Nothing special happens on the first hand, and Will takes the trick by playing the highest club. Then he leads the next hand with a four of spades, hoping to smoke out the queen. Everyone is nervous because you don't want to take the hand with the queen — that means you get thirteen points against you!

It's too early in the game to shoot the moon, and everyone squeaks by with playing lower spades.

Richard had painted the trick by playing a heart. Now that hearts are broken, the following hands have a lot of them thrown, with people getting penalty points as they take the tricks for that hand.

Scores are adding up for us players, and comments are thrown across the table.

"I wonder where that queen of spades is hiding," says Richard. No one has thrown her yet, and we're getting to the end, not many cards left in our hands.

Will tries hard to cover up his poker face, but most of us notice his expression and figure he's got the queen.

Shooting the moon won't happen in this hand, because hearts have already been played (you have to take all the hearts and queen as tricks in one hand to shoot the moon). But he can still do some damage by putting one of us over 100 points and ending the game.

We play one more hand, and Will wins—even though I'm complaining like everyone else, inside I'm grinning. It's so great to see him—and us—having fun again, laughing and cutting up and joking around. *We've finally arrived at our new life.*

WILL: FREEDOM

Freedom is the oxygen of the soul.

— Moshe Dayan

I'd been going to college at Eastern Montana College for a year. I had to make endless arrangements for someone to drive me back and forth to class. The vocational rehab man had helped us get an old Corvair van with no windows in the back of it. He also found a welding shop to build some metal ramps for loading me from the rear of the van, and they took out all the seats except the driver's and front passenger seats. That left enough room in the back to wheel me in and tie my chair down. It was mobility, I admit, but I was uncomfortable riding in the thing. My chair sat up too high for me to see out the front windshield, and the van didn't have any side windows. It was scary back there, lurching side to side in the dark. My brothers had rigged up a canvas sling that hung from the metal roof of the van. I'd slip my arm into it and hang on as hard as I could so I wouldn't get so car sick from pitching around.

College days were a challenge. In the wintertime, the streets and sidewalks were stacked with snow, and pushing my wheels through it to get to class was nearly impossible. I had to rely on my classmates many times to push me through the stuff because I didn't have the strength in my arms to muscle my way through. Besides, if I got lopsided on a rut, I could tip my chair over and disaster could result. In addition to that, one of my business classes was on the third floor of Benson Hall with no elevator in the building. I'd leave class early to wait at the bottom of the stairs, asking guys if they'd help haul me upstairs. I had black tape that marked the spots where they'd have to grab the chair. Most of them were really good about it; I'd have four guys pick me up and cart me all the way up. The reverse would happen after class. I'd have to leave a few minutes early to wait at the top of the stairs. I got real good at convincing people to help me, being funny and saying things like, "The girls are going to see how macho you are, hauling this two-hundred-pound cripple down the stairs," and, "I'll bet you can't take me all the way to the top without stopping."

But a lot of times, there wasn't any help. That's when my big brother Dean would have to leave work and drive up to get me. My heart would race when he had to take me down those stairs by himself. One slip, one wrong move, and both of us could end up at the bottom of three flights in an instant. We'd both get our heart rates up trying to deal with that.

Then there was the time the football players were hauling me down the stairs and just above the landing, they dropped me. One boy slipped and knocked everybody off balance. I didn't topple out of my chair, but my left rim was bent, and I couldn't move. I had to get one of them to call Dean and he came right over. He had to take the wheel off and prop me up on a low bench. He took it to his shop and got it trued up again. A couple hours later, I was back in business. I relied on him a lot those days, and I'll always be grateful that he'd moved back here when he got out of the Air Force. I don't know what I'd have done without him. When he and Charley, my sister-in-law, had their first baby, it was a boy. They named him Will. My eyes went teary when they told me.

I wanted freedom. I wanted it more than anything else at that point. For four long years, I'd had to wait until someone else was ready to do something for me. Dress me. Drive me. Empty my leg bag full of urine. Get me out of my wheelchair and into bed. Bathe me.

Then rehab found a '72 Ford Econoline van with an automatic transmission and windows all around. They decided to build some hand controls so I could learn to drive it myself. One lever was the gas, the other was the brakes. They'd spent hours testing it, making sure it was safe to operate, and making sure I could grasp the hand controls easily and respond instantly so I could maneuver in traffic.

Although this was a big step for me, because now I could actually drive myself around, I still needed someone to haul me up and down the metal ramps. That's when Rehab Bob and I started working on the people over at DVR to rig up a hydraulic platform. We had the summer to get it done before I started school again in the fall.

We got the specialists over at D&G Electric and the welder's shop to start building the platform. The idea was similar to the automatic lifts you see on the back of delivery trucks. The kind that unfolds and lowers to the ground; then it lifts back up the level of the truck bed, allowing the delivery man to roll his hand cart back into the truck. The concept was the same for my rig, so they got started on building the thing. We needed some special controls set up for me to be able to operate it. There was a set of controls on the outside of the van, along the side of it at a level where I could reach them. I could open the cover and flip the toggle switches with the back of my hand. The double doors would open, and then the lift would unfold and lower the platform to the ground. I would roll onto the platform, lock my wheels with the hand levers on the chair, and throw the toggle switch to raise the platform. At the top, I'd wheel into the rear of the van, stopping partway to throw another switch on the inside wall that would fold the platform into the van, and close the doors behind it.

I'd roll into the driver's spot, where the welders had built small "wheel wells" into the floor of the van. These metal indentations allowed me to lower my back wheels down from the level of the van floor. To lock my chair down and secure it while I was driving, I would lift up a long metal rod with a small cross-piece at the bottom and turn it sideways so the cross-piece would slip over the rim of my back wheel. I'd drop the rod, and the cross-piece would fall into an indentation in the floor, much like a sliding bolt on a door. I wasn't exactly seat-belted in, but I was stable and secure. I no longer had to worry about my wheelchair lurching side to side with the motion of the van.

For the entire month of June, every spare minute was spent on the phone with the shop or with the mechanics out in the driveway. They'd bring the van over to test their latest invention and make modifications when we needed them. The weather was usually warm and comfortable, so I'd wheel down the ramp from the back door and hang out in the screened patio between the house and the garage, waiting for them to pull up in the driveway. Then I'd wheel out to the driveway to see what they had in store for me, their guinea pig. Many summer evenings were spent shooting the breeze with the mechanics while they tinkered with the van.

In the meantime, my grandma heard about what we were trying to do, and sent me some money, quite a lot actually, to help outfit the van. That's when we decided to see about having the RV shop do a custom-build on the van's body. The Econoline's engine casing intruded so far inside the van at the front that I had to sit far to the left of the steering wheel in order to get my legs and the wheelchair underneath. It put me in such an awkward position that my neck and arms would ache from craning sideways to manipulate the steering wheel. So the guys thought if we could keep the infrastructure they'd already built with the hydraulics and controls, and just give the van a new shell, it would solve this dilemma for me. The RV dealer agreed to take on the project and began building it right away. We even ordered an extra-large front windshield and big side windows to give me maximum range of sight.

Dean and Gordy got involved with the project too. They'd come over in the evenings to inspect the progress and jump in whenever the mechanic needed a hand at something.

A month later, the freshly painted tin trailer with monster windows stood in the driveway, beckoning me to take her for a spin.

On test drive day, Gordy took me over to the high school parking lot to practice. We jockeyed around while Gordy pulled the driver's seat post out and set it aside in the back of the van. I rolled forward to the driver's spot to get in position and locked my wheelchair down. Grabbing the suicide knob with my left hand and squeezing the gas hand control with my right, we pitched forward. I eased off the control too much and we sputtered to a stop. I started to get the hang of it a few minutes later, when I noticed what looked like a curb. I squeezed the brake control so hard that Gordy got thrown forward into the dashboard, spraining his finger when he reached out to break the impact. "Jesus, Will, you're going to get a ticket driving like this!" he yelled.

What better way to recapture my pre-quadriplegic life than four tires and a steering wheel — the invitation of the open road, the blast of wind through the driver's window, the pure "windshield time" that I so craved.

It had been four years since I actually drove an automobile. Four years from the rollover that broke my neck to the day I sat behind the wheel again, in control of the machine that could take me anywhere I wanted to go. A road trip to wherever. To the grocery store. To school. To visit a friend. The destination didn't matter — what mattered was the fact that I didn't have to rely on someone else to drive me there.

I'd dreamed of this day ever since I was imprisoned on the rotating hospital bed that reminded ever so much that I could never drive a car again.

Today, here I was. Behind the wheel again. It felt like home. It felt natural. I'd driven farm tractors for Lawrence since I was twelve years old. I'd driven my big brother's '56 Chevy Bel-Air sedan in Walden. (He was pretty stingy with turning the key over to me, though.) I thought of the numerous times when I "borrowed" my mom's car in the middle of the night and cruised around Cody without her knowing it.

But this. This was a miracle. To have my own means of mobility, with a hydraulic lift to get me into the thing, and hand controls attached to the steering wheel for the gas and brakes. The "suicide knob" on the steering wheel let me grasp the wheel with my crippled hand in order to navigate the beast.

I could wheel myself into place behind the controls and lock my wheelchair down. In those days, the HP would question this setup, even though seat belts weren't mandatory. I did it anyway and took the chance on getting a ticket if I was ever pulled over.

I was wildly elated with my newfound freedom. I made up any excuse to drive somewhere, and sometimes didn't even bother with an excuse, saying only that I needed to get out of the house and get some fresh air.

Of course, I ran into some obstacles. Like pumping gas. I couldn't manipulate the hoses or pump handles or even get the gas cap off to pump my own gas. So I always had to find a full-service place to do it for me. When I went shopping or to movies, I had to park strategically so I'd have room for the lift to go down in the back, and room enough along the side of the van to get to the control panel. After I had the van for about four months, I discovered another obstacle. The battery would die and I'd get stranded time after time, not able to open the van doors or lower the platform to get out of the van. Eventually, my brothers installed an extra bank of batteries to handle the electrical demand.

But I knew this was a huge step toward independence, and it encouraged me to start dreaming about what else I could do on my own, to build a life of my own again.

I learned even more about self-sufficiency when I went to Seattle that winter. I'd been having trouble with my internal catheter, so again Rehab Bob got me in touch with the hospital in Seattle that specialized in paralysis victims. They flew me out and I stayed for six weeks. It was over Christmas break, and I did miss some school the beginning of the semester, but it was worth it. They switched me to an external catheter, and the sweats, fever, and chills subsided almost immediately. They showed me self-care methods, like using a satin sheet on my bed and arm slings so I could sit up by myself and move myself on the bed, changing positions often to avoid bedsores. They taught me to use my arms and do "push-ups" on my wheelchair armrests to relieve the pressure when sitting in my chair for long periods of time.

Mom flew out for a visit and to be with me on Christmas Day. She was amazed at my progress and all that I'd learned. We both were thrilled that I finally had a chance of moving toward independent living. That's when we started talking about a possible change of residence—moving to Phoenix, a place where the snow and ice wouldn't keep me from being mobile all year round.

It meant moving away from my brothers and little sister, but it sure was appealing. Mom was willing to move there with me to get set up, and besides, she told me, she was tired of the cold, hard winters herself.

BEVERLY: INDEPENDENCE DAY

If at first, you don't succeed, take the tax loss.

— Kirk Kirkpatrick

We've lived in Arizona for nearly seven years. Things have settled down for both Will and me. He's bought his own house, and he has a life of his own now. I have my home too, and it is a good life I live these days. I have friends to square dance with every week, a couple of cousins who live here that I can visit frequently, and for the first time in nearly two decades, I can live my own life on my own terms.

I'm happy for the most part, except the work. I'm tired of answering to bosses, to taking their slights and tolerating their bad moods. I need to be on my own.

When we first arrived here, I had to find a job and find one quick. We'd used every last cent we had from the insurance settlement to get us moved and set up with a house for Will. We'd found one that he could lease for a year with an option to buy at the end of that year. So, we had living quarters figured out. But we needed income too. I started my job search. I set up my trusty IBM Selectric typewriter and began composing:

To Whom It May Concern:

I am seeking work at your establishment as a bookkeeper. I have many years of experience which I can discuss with you if you wish to interview me.

My education includes the International Accountants Society-home study courses completed in 1972; Bell & Howell Schools-correspondence-90 lessons in accounting elements, general, basic cost, corporation accounting, and basic and public auditing; and, yearly IRS income tax seminars.

I prefer to work within a ten-mile radius of Sunnyslope/Dunlap/Cave Creek, and your location meets with this criteria.

It will be very much appreciated to hear from you, even though you may not desire to interview me. This request stems from the frustration of never

knowing if my resume is received and
not knowing your reasoning of it and
whether my qualifications meet your
needs.

Thank you,
Beverly Pearson

The only times I can be reached by
telephone are: Before 7:45 a.m., between
11:30 a.m. and 12:30 p.m., or after 5 p.m.

I finally landed a job at the American Heart Association as their accountant. It was a good, solid job and the people were nice to me. I especially liked Donna, the executive director. We'd have long talks about streamlining the accounting system, and she let me try out my ideas.

But the pay was low and we were barely squeaking by on monthly bills. As much as I hated to leave a job that I liked, I had to strike out again to try to find a better paying job. After I left AHA, I took on a series of accounting jobs from construction companies to a convalescent center on East Roosevelt, and eventually a food distributorship.

After another ten years of this kind of employment, I was simply tired of running my tail off for someone else and not getting paid what I was worth. So, I cooked up a plan to start my own business. I had a deep background of working for many different kinds of companies, from automobile repair shops and service stations to doctor's offices and oil companies. Phoenix had a wealth of small companies in need of an accountant. I started making the rounds, walking in to businesses and asking to speak to the owner. After about six weeks, I'd landed a dozen accounts. I knew I needed more than that, but it was a start. That's when I created Alves Accounting: a full-service bookkeeping—accounting—taxes enterprise. I ended up with a lot of payroll customers too.

One of my favorite clients was Sabinder, an East Indian immigrant and the owner of PRK Automotive on Cave Creek Road. Once a month, I'd make my rounds to clients, hauling boxes and envelopes filled with ledgers and receipts and checks written for them to sign. My trusty old Ford LTD had lots of room for storage, so I could make ten to twelve stops in a day.

Sabinder was very respectful of me and my expertise. But I learned that he didn't always get right down to business. He was never in a hurry to send me on my way, and he always took time to start our conversation with some light chitchat and banter about personal topics to catch up on the goings-on of my family. Although my stop at his gas station always took longer than my other clients, it was the highlight of my day.

He loved my Ford LTD. He would carry his box full of receipts for the month out to my car, and as I opened the cavernous trunk, his remarks would run something like this:

"Mrs. Alves, the automobile you drive is most beautiful. In my country, it would be a display of wealth as you drive the streets. You would be considered royalty in my homeland." He'd run his hand along the cloth top, then bend to see inside to check out the luxurious, tufted upholstered seats.

"This is most excellent." He beamed at me.

"Why, thank you, Sabinder," I replied, smiling at him. "She's nothing special, but she's reliable and she gets me where I need to go."

"*She?* You have a name for your automobile?" His eyes lit up. He was curious about the independent American woman who personified her vehicle.

"Well, I never thought about it before," I said. "But now that I think of it, I guess I gave my car feminine characteristics. I've found women to be more reliable than men, generally."

"Interesting perspective, Mrs. Alves." Sabinder peered at me over the top of his eyeglasses. "I have found that to be true too. But does she have a name?"

"Well, I guess I call her Gertrude most times when I'm driving around. You know, like, '*Come on, Gertrude, you're a strong gal, let's get these accounts delivered on time today.'*"

That brought a broad smile to his dark brown face. Then he lowered his box of receipts into the car's trunk, turned to me, pressing his hands together, and bowed slightly.

"Until next month then, Mrs. Alves," he said. "I wish for you and Gertrude prosperous times."

"Same to you, Sabinder. Thank you."

He was my favorite customer by far. I still think of him today and wish him well.

WILL: BLIND DATE

"In the valley of the blind, the one-eyed man is king."

— August Wilson, *Gem of the Ocean*

A l slouched in his chair, tapped his cane against the unforgiving linoleum. His head swayed slightly from side to side. Sweat trickled down his cheeks and dribbled into his lap. The tiny, overloaded air conditioner whirred overhead in a futile attempt to reduce the Arizona heat to boiling point. His shorts clung to his skin and glued him to the plastic chair. We waited for him to start.

"I can't just walk into a room and make eye contact. And I can't smile at somebody when we meet walking down my street."

"Yeah," Joe piped in. "A lot of times when I ride the bus, I wear mismatched shoes just to try to get a comment from a girl." His goatee quivered just an instant, and his chin jutted forward. I glanced around. No one else seemed to catch his movements.

I prompted Joe to tell us why he would do that.

"I'm just trying to engineer any kind of social contact, especially if she has a pretty voice."

"So you're saying it's love at *no* sight, huh?" As usual, I cracked a joke to cover up my own fears.

"Yeah, well, you don't have to be a prick about it," Al sneered at me. "I think 'sighties' like you might be more disabled than guys like me. What about your affair with Sheila? You chased her for her good looks, but you found out her beauty was only skin deep. She really took you down, man."

His jab struck home. "Touché, partner. I shouldn't have tried such a low blow. I have to remember that we're all in this pile of crap together." Weeks ago I'd told them about my "Sheila" chapter, attempting to share some of my own dilemmas and maybe guide them to a few better choices than I'd made.

We were in the middle of one of our weekly sessions. I'd seen and heard dozens of stories from men who were disabled but who wanted a normal life, especially in the romance department. The subject came up about trying to date if you're blind. Making that first contact, the starting point for any relationship, was next to impossible for these two men, who'd both had accidents while they were in their twenties.

What are you supposed to do when you have no way of knowing if the person sitting next to you was the one you sat next to yesterday or if they work three floors up in your building? Just like the men I counseled, I was desperate to date again.

Joe's comment about Sheila tossed me into a mire of melancholy memories. It was close to my birthday in February 1983; I was going to turn thirty-four that year — seventeen years lived as a "quad," and I finally felt like I was on top for once. I'd been bragging to Gordy and our cousin Gage about the Candy Store Stripper Club over on Cave Creek, how the place was perfect for me to get a front row seat. Anytime I rolled through the door in my wheelchair, the crowds parted and gave way to the best seat in the house. There was one girl — Desert Flame — who always danced there on Thursday nights. I made a point of being there every week.

"Yeah, Sheila, she's one of the Risqué Kitty Strippers. Her stage name is Desert Flame. She's built like a brick house." I was trying to impress Gage, my cousin, the guy who could get any girl he wanted into the sack. "And I'm going to score with her — maybe tonight!"

"How're you gonna do that, Will, when you can't figure out when you're gonna get a boner?!" That bastard Gage, he was right — how *was* I going to pull that one off?

"I'll just tell her what to do — you know, give her instructions, and I can tell when I'm ready to go. I still need it as much as you do, so just mind your potatoes, you turd bucket."

Gordy would go with me on a lot of those Thursday

nights. Like Gage, he was built like our Basque ancestors. Heavy and solid with wide shoulders and slim hips;
oversized forearms and large hands; the forehead straight
with only a bump at the brow bridge; and a slightly thin-
ning hairline, but not so much as to cause alarm in young
women. I had more of my German grandpa's barrel chest,
a high-set jawline, and a smaller nose. I stood six-foot-
two, and he was a wimpy five-foot-ten. I knew I was the
more handsome one, but he attracted the girls and they
fluttered around him like moths to a flame. When Gordy
was in the room, I faded into the woodwork, and the girls
barely glanced my way. It had always pissed me off.

Gage and my brother had "secretly" planned my
birthday party, so I couldn't get too pissed at them. I
knew we were going bar-hopping to celebrate, but I did
a double-take when we pulled into the parking lot at
the Candy Store. I wasn't that interested because it was
Friday night and my fiery Desert Flame only danced on
Thursdays.

"This place is gonna be pretty boring—why're we
here *tonight*?" I unlocked my wheelchair from the van's
metal braces, rolled onto the lift, and pushed the "down"
button with my knuckle.

As soon as I wheeled off the lift, Gage blindfolded me.
"You'll find out soon enough, Chubby!"

I cringed at Gage's reference to the nickname stepfather number three had bestowed on me. "Fine," I said.
"But don't call me that in front of the ladies. They think

my name is Jack Lord."

The boys wheeled me inside, and dense feet scuffled behind me. Startled by a sudden and jerky boost from four sets of invisible hands, my levitation quickly ended, and I knew I was on the stage where the girls danced.

The voice glided from the speaker next to me, crooning a German-inflected burlesque tune. The blindfold, loosened by invisible fingers, fell into my lap. I was center stage with my fantasy girl staring into my eyes. If I could have fallen backward at that point, I would have!

Wrapping her silky scarf around my head, she twirled away from me, pulling the scarf with her, then turning to see if I was looking. I was. More than looking. I was panting. "Ohhhh, wow!" It was me, but it wasn't my voice.

The crooner continued, lulling the two of us into a love dance. Guitar notes and the singer's voice barely penetrated my consciousness. She floated back across the stage to me, coiling her body around me, then retreating behind me. She grabbed the handles of my chair, twirling me around to face her again, and positioned herself on my lap.

Then, a startling techno tempo and wavy organ notes reverberated in my ears. She jumped up, shed even more flimsy underwear, and gyrated around the maypole a few feet in front of me. Teasing, seductive; I was losing my mind with desire. Sweat beaded up on my forehead. My glasses slid down my nose. It annoyed me but only for a second. As soon as I pushed them up, my vision cleared, and she was doing a thing with the splits only vertical along the pole. *Is that possible?* I tried to turn my head sideways to watch the opposite direction of each leg. The disco ball threw lasers of light all over the stage and into the audience. Oh yeah, the audience. I forgot there was anyone else there besides the two of us.

A low, soothing love song lured me back to her. I halfway heard the lyrics, something about touching me and things starting to grow, then making love. Woodwinds, bells, flute, and a drumbeat rhythm mesmerized me. She engulfed me in her gaze, deepening the trance. Lowering herself to my lap, she leaned in close, wrapped her arms around my neck, her delicate tongue in my ear. Catapulted into instant nirvana, I sensed we were the only two humans on earth.

She whispered, "I want to be with you."

I whispered back, "When?"

I must have been insane to think someone like Sheila would hang around with a cripple like me. After she pawned some of my tools and things out of the garage that she knew I wouldn't miss right away, she vanished back into the Phoenix nightlife just as fast as she had materialized before me that night at the bar.

For weeks after she left, I'd hole up in my den, poring over the dozens of mushy cards she'd habitually left propped at my computer, where she knew I'd find them. First, "I'm just glad I'm learning about love with you." *Love, Sheila* Then, "Even if I told you 'I love you' a million times a day...it still wouldn't be enough to tell you what's in my heart." *Our Christmases can only get better!* *Love, Sheila* "Take my love and hold it closely to your heart…And I will give you all that's mine to give." *Love, Sheila* "Once in a blue moon you meet someone incredible. I'm glad I met you." *I love you! Sheila*

With each reading of each generic greeting card, her endearments scribbled like an afterthought, my grief oozed out of my pores like the stench of garlic after a big Italian meal. It permeated my every waking moment and most of my dream life too. I was an emotional wreck — empty, alone, and terrified. There was no second chance for me, a quad in a damn wheelchair.

Mom became my personal counselor then, encouraging me to date again. My first attempts were pitiful. I even stooped to writing to a girl through an anonymous newspaper ad:

```
    I am a citified country boy. I was
raised on farms and ranches in Colorado
and Wyoming. My values are more tradi-
tional because of my upbringing. Because
of my education (a master's degree) and a
physical disability, I feel I am a flex-
ible, open, understanding, sensitive man. I
cried when I saw Beaches and Rain Man. I
am the second of four children and have
a very strong, loving family.
    My curiosity gets me back to you again!
```

What kinds of movies do you enjoy? Who are your favorite actors and actresses? What is your favorite color? Where is your favorite getaway? Why? What kind of work do you do? Do you have children? Where were you raised?

I have an answering machine and use it to screen calls while I'm writing or if I'm at the library. If you call (and I hope you will) and you get my answering machine, please leave your name, number, and say that I wrote to you through Single Scenes. If I'm home, I answer in a few seconds. If not, I'll call you ASAP.

I know you will receive a lot of letters, so I've enclosed an envelope for you to return my picture if you choose not to respond to me.

I wish you the best and hope we can meet.

Sincerely,
Will Alves

Her answer came back in my self-addressed, stamped envelope: *Thank you for your wonderful letter, but of the thirty-three letters I received I have found someone that I want to pursue a relationship with. Sincerely, NB 7564*

After a couple of months and mounds of rejection

letters from women like NB 7564, my hopes of success in the Single Scenes plummeted. I needed a new tack. Several weeks later, I was at Salon Mystique on East Camelback Road for my haircut. It was geared toward women, but it was the only one I could find close to home that was wheelchair accessible. I wheeled into the lobby to wait for Gina, my stylist. A magazine lay half-hidden on the side table: "COMPLETE WOMAN, For All—"

I fished it from the table and read the rest of the title: "—The Women You Are." I sandwiched it between my knuckles and laid it on my lap, hoping I could get the pages open without my hand brace.

Inside the front cover, the print blazed a message into my brain: "Wanted: male contributors. We are looking for the man's point of view. Are you the man for us?"

October 1, 1991

Susan Handy, Managing Editor
Associated Publications, Inc.
1165 N. Clark -
Chicago, IL 60610

Dear Editor:

Have you ever dated a man with a disability? Men with disabilities have the same qualities as other men. Many of those qualities are enhanced because of the disability-sensitivity, caring, giving, accepting, depth, maturity, responsibility, and the ability to communicate. Just because they can't feel below their neck doesn't mean they don't have feelings. Too many single women overlook the possibility of having a quality relationship with a man because he uses a wheelchair or white cane.

Women of the 1990s are searching for long-lasting, stable, mature relationships based on a man's intrinsic qualities. Men with disabilities want strong, independent, sincere women to share their lives. Some amazing relationships have been built on this very stuff.

In a 1200-word piece, I interview five women, including a television news anchor, a recreational therapist, and a computer systems analyst—even an attorney and an architect—who dated and later married men with disabilities.

Will you take a look at my article?

Sincerely yours,
Will Alves

Excerpt: DATE A DISABLED MAN? CONSIDER IT!!!
By Will Alves

Julie's audience loves to watch her bright smile and sparkling eyes as she brings us the nightly news on TV. She's upbeat and bouncy, a real "catch" in the dating world. When I approached her and asked if we could talk about whether she would date a disabled man, she told me this:

"I actually dated a man who uses a wheelchair, and he became my husband last year. When we first started dating, I was intrigued and open to the possibilities. I wanted to see where it would lead. But he was anxious about dating me, and his trepidation showed up right away. Even though we'd gone out at least a half-dozen times, he hadn't tried to kiss me good night or even hold my hand. I'd driven him home several times and we spent hours sitting in my car talking, but he hadn't invited me in to see his apartment.

"I knew I was going to have to make the first move if we were ever going to explore the possibility of a romantic relationship. I told him how much he made me laugh, and that I loved his wry sense of humor. He'd say things like, 'I'm the wheel deal,' or 'Hey, I don't know if you're into hiking Mount Everest, but if you are, go for it. I'll hang out at base camp and keep the tent warm for you!' I tried to let him know he was attractive to me and that I didn't even figure the wheelchair into the

equation. Once he kissed me, that was it — I was hooked. I had a crush on this guy. We spent every spare minute together for the next year. When he proposed, my answer was a swift YES!

"So you see, his disability was not a deterrent for me — in fact, I'm getting pretty kick-ass at getting the wheelchair folded up and in my car when we go places."

I never heard back from Susan Handy, the magazine editor. But something shifted for me. My willingness to put myself out there again, to view myself as a desirable, mature man who ladies long to meet, created a magnetism. Women started to approach me. Kay, the waitress at the diner on 67th, asked me out for coffee. Glenda, our receptionist at DES, flirted with me for two weeks, then invited me out to a movie. Then there was the short road trip to Flagstaff one Saturday with Sherry.

None of these dates led to anything, but it boosted my confidence and helped ease my fears of rejection. I admit that I was intimidated by the prospect of being anyone's boyfriend again. I realized that I actually feared things would go well with one of these ladies, and then I'd screw it up again somehow. My inherent love of women won out in the end, and I continued to date. That's when I met Josephine.

BEVERLY: SETTING THE COURSE

The pessimist complains about the wind; the optimist expects it to change; the realist adjusts the sails.

— William Arthur Ward

Will and I had been living in Phoenix for ten years when he hired Cora Stiles, a care attendant. Cora was a lovely woman and she was very kind to my son. We struck up a friendship too, even though she was twenty years younger than I was. I ended up spending many evenings at Will's house, having dinner and visiting at the kitchen table with her afterward. I found out that she had been trained in astrology and was actually AFA certified, but Cora was quite humble about her expertise in the complications of setting up a mathematically correct natal zodiac chart.

Both Will and I were curious about the charting and begged her to develop ours for us. In fact, my son and

I were avid readers of our daily horoscopes. Over the years we'd had ongoing discussions about our signs, and because we ended up in a closer relationship than most sons and moms, we wondered how compatible we were.

She finally agreed to our project. Several weeks later, she presented us with her reports, meticulously typed and several dozen pages long. We sat at the kitchen table, poring over the pages with Cora reassuring us that our signs were indeed compatible.

She explained that Will's birth date and time created a "Grand Air Trine" with his sun, moon, and rising signs, a very lucky aspect.

"This trine helps you to be a natural in dealing with any mental tasks. Will, you're highly intellectual, and learning is both fascinating and easy for you," Cora said.

"Beverly, like Will, earth is lacking in your horoscope," she continued. "Your sun is in Leo, of course, and your moon is in Aquarius; your ascendant sign is in Libra. You have a strong influence from the air signs too."

Cora pulled the pages from both our reports, showing us that the deepest value we share is the value of individuality, and that this creates a strong connection for us. She pointed out that, even though we are solidly compatible, some things could tend to get in our way. We needed to watch for challenges in trust and being truthful with each other.

"But," said Cora, "the good thing is that you are both

heroes in your own way. You will be unstoppable when you find a common cause, and you will create an incredible force that can change anything."

I took those typed pages as gospel. *"As a Leo born on August 22nd, 1926, you are sociable and confident. You would jump straight into anything that involves a change in your life and in your routine.*

"Some things are quite contrasting in your personality, such as how you can be both jealous and indifferent, exactly during the moments that are considered of highest intensity."

The pages revealed the true me: *"Those born on this day are self-confident and often so actively engaged in as many endeavors at the same time that it is almost impossible to keep up with them. Leo people are by definition communicative but also inspire respect rather than friendliness and are also emotionally strong."* The report went on: *"People born on August 22 are convincing and persistent when they want to achieve a goal. They need to feel in control so they are sure they can do whatever they want without any setbacks from others."*

Of course, that was me! I read on:

"Those born in August are outgoing and adventurous. August 22 Zodiac people are perseverant and strong-willed. You are enterprising and ambitious just like a true Leo and courageous warriors just as Mars makes them be. Being born on the 22nd day of the month shows efficiency, confidence, logic and stubbornness."

Next, I read about my negative traits: *"Leos are controlling and patronizing and they never seem to take a break from* showing themselves in a boastful light. They often dramatize things a lot and they are never to say when they are at fault, despite everything being blatantly clear."

The report went on: "They are a person of extremes in love, and sometimes with this attitude they are prone to disappointment. They are likely to fall in love at a young age and have many interactions with different kinds of people. They are most compatible with those born on 1st, 8th, 10th, 17th, 19th, 26th and 28th.

"The color for Leo natives born on August 22 is orange. This hue denotes healing and high stimulation coupled with vitality. The zodiac color should be used in items of clothing or objects in the house. Those with orange as sign color are creative, optimistic persons for whom the world is a stage, and they have so many things to show. They need to socialize, be accepted and respected as part of a group. It is hard to gain their trust but once achieved you have a friend for life. They are the most helpful and compassionate friends."

I read the last page of my report:

"Leo has true inner dignity and grace that lets her carry her misfortunes with courage. The warm yellow rays of her cheerful hope deepen to orange in sunset's glow and her nights are bright with a thousand stars."

This is me, this is who I am. Beverly Faye Pearson.

BEVERLY: DO SI DO

It's when you're in a circle at a party in a barn
that square dancing comes to mind.

— Anthony T. Hincks

After Everett came home from the Navy, in the winter of 1948, he and I, along with four other couples, got together most every Saturday night at an old abandoned house on Cerro Summit to square dance. We had one square of adults, and another square of kids. Two of the men were callers. They took turns. Sometimes we had a fiddle player, but when we had no live music, our friend Hank had a collection of records in two metal boxes that he'd bring, along with his record player, speakers, and calling microphone. Some records had the tune on one side and the tune with calling on the other so folks could still dance even if no local live caller was available. Hank taught himself to call by listening to these recordings of

246

professionals calling. He'd then write out the dances by hand and, while taking long walks, practice calling them until he knew them by heart.

We'd spend all winter long up there doing that. And then when we got together for bigger dances at the community center in Montrose, we'd dance all night long.

In those days, only men called, so it went something like *"Walk all around your right-hand lady, Seesaw your pretty little taw..."*

Or he referred to the woman as *"your little red hen."* He'd also call to promenade "Indian-style," meaning single file.

Hank was really good at changing the calls too. You didn't know what was coming next. He was my favorite caller.

He improvised a lot, which is tough because you have to remember who began where and with whom, and somehow get everyone back home—and with their partner. But when you can pull it off, there's nothing more fun. We loved it because we never knew what was coming next.

Not only that, but Hank had enthusiasm and was relaxed. You could tell he was having fun. When we heard Hank call, we knew it would be a fun night.

At times, his improvisation could get downright goofy. I remember one in particular from Hank's calling: *"Walk right up and bend the line, then swing around with ole Frankenstein."* Not only did this cause an uproar, it also prompted us dancers to listen closely to him at all times.

Years later, when Will and I moved to Phoenix, I joined a square dance club over on Sunny Slope near my house. Almost every Friday night, I'd hop in my big old Ford LTD and drive over to the Holiday Spa Mobile Home Park. Most of those nights, I'd end up with Harvey as my dancing partner.

We became a regular "couple" but dancing was as far as it went with us. I didn't feel the spark of romance with him at all, even though I always got the impression he would've liked things to get more serious. Harvey was a nice man, and he respected me. He never tried to get frisky with me or cross that line. We were good friends and we sure cut it up on the dance floor!

WILL: DREAM GIRL, ROUND THREE

"When you're going through hell — keep going."

— Winston Churchill

Mom had gone square dancing at the Squaw Mountain Community Center with her friends Betty and Herb most every week over the past year, and one Sunday, they invited us over for dinner. Their daughter Josephine was there too. They introduced us and right away I liked her. She took my hand in hers, and her mouth skewed into a gentle, crooked smile as she scrunched her pixie nose. Corn-silk hair framed her Teutonic cheekbones, and her Dodger-blue eyes sparkled behind the oval wire-rimmed glasses. I wondered how long I could stare at her without her thinking me strange.

I regained my senses. "What books do you like to read?" I wanted to set her up for some of my standard jokes.

"Oh, let's see. I just got done reading *Family Album* by Danielle Steel." Distracted by her glistening, luscious lips, I was mesmerized by the way she formed her words and puckered them to the side as she spoke.

"I-I don't know that one—what's it about?" The only thing I knew was that every one of my female friends read the new Danielle Steel book the minute it hit the check-out line at the grocery store.

"It's the story of Faye Price, who started out as a Hollywood actress and became one of the first female directors. But the real story for her was her family life—her marriage, separations and reconciliations with her husband, the struggles they go through to raise their kids, and then in the end, they come through stronger."

"That sounds like a great story. Want to hear what I've been reading?" I was under control now, and ready to deliver my punch lines.

"Sure! I don't know many men who actually like to read!"

"Well, I'm not your typical man."

"So, what have you been reading?"

"Last week, I finished *Under the Bleachers* by Seymour Butts."

"Huh?"

"And the week before that, I read *Yellow River* by I.P. Freely."

"*Gross!* Okay, Mr. Smarty Pants. I know your game now!" She giggled. I smiled and nodded.

"Time for supper!" called Josephine's mom. Following my nose and the amazing aromas wafting from the next room, I spun my wheelchair and rolled into the kitchen with Josephine shuffling behind me.

The table was set up as if it was Thanksgiving. On top of the real tablecloth (no chintzy plastic like we used at home), fall flowers in a copper vase were framed by expensive china and gleaming silverware.

"Wow! This is beautiful, Mrs. Ackerman." I felt awkward and regretted not dressing up a bit more.

"Oh, it vas nuth-ing, my dear boy," she replied, her words reflecting the Germanic flavor of her heritage. "Und call me Betty, please! We're happy to have you and your mother here with us tonight!"

Between bites of slow-cooked pork roast with sauerkraut and roasted vegetables, we talked about the square dances, my work, and Josephine's job. When the subject of reruns of *Leave It To Beaver* came up, we all cracked up with Herb's rendition of the episode about Wally's hair comb. Wally gets sucked in by some ridiculous fad at school, and the parents have to gently point out to him how ridiculous he seems. In this case, Wally begins combing his hair very oddly, and while his dad is willing to give him time to figure out how stupid he looks, June is driven increasingly up the wall by her son's appearance.

"You've never done something that silly, have you, Will?" Josephine was baiting me, but I was cool.

"Sure I have—but you'll never hear about it!" I gloated.

Josephine was antsy to pry for details when Mrs. Ackerman (*plees! Call me Betty!*) brought out dessert. She called it "Topfenstrudel." I picked up only the strudel part, so I knew it was going to be delicious. In a June Cleaver-style apron and a glossy smile, Mrs. Ackerman ladled it onto warm plates.

"If you can cook just a fraction as good as your mom," I leered at Josephine, "I bet you could write your ticket for any boyfriend you choose."

Her blush told me it was time to change the subject. "Shall we play some cards with these old folks?"

"No." Josephine stood up and started clearing the dishes. "Let's play Yahtzee," she said over her shoulder as she took the dishes to the sink, refilling her wineglass not-so-discreetly at the kitchen counter.

Mrs. Ackerman followed Josephine. Under her breath, I heard her say, "You've had three drinks. You know, Josephine, it's not good to be a three-drink girl. You don't want to cross that line." I caught Josephine rolling her eyes. She reminded her mom that drinking in moderation was actually good for her health.

"In fact," Josephine said as she turned toward her, "alcohol is thought to be so effective in helping people live longer and stay mentally sharp that some experts have suggested that aging teetotalers start a daily habit. Hey, maybe *you* should drink more!"

Mrs. Ackerman wiped her hand on her apron and stalked out of the kitchen. Herb offered me another beer, which I readily accepted. We exchanged glances. Boy, this was going to be *some show.*

We rigged up the Yahtzee cup with some rubber bands so that I could shake and throw the dice. We played until close to midnight, me being the winner of most of the rounds by throwing the most Yahtzees. The grumbling from the others made me feel superior. I tried not to gloat, but it sure was great to come out on top for once.

"Well, I guess it's time to collect my winnings and be on my way." I beamed. Everyone groaned.

Josephine walked with me to the van. I rolled over to the control panel and flipped the first toggle switch. The van doors popped apart slightly; then the hydraulics took over and they opened up. I flipped the second switch and the metal ramp descended to the driveway.

Intrigued by the lift mechanisms, Josephine asked, "How do the doors and ramp work? Are they electric? Can you lock them so robbers can't break in?"

The questions came in such fast succession, I couldn't get a word in to try to explain.

"Here. Let me show you," I finally broke in and stopped her barrage.

I demonstrated how I could lock the control panel with a key anchored into a large wooden T-shaped handle, which I kept tethered to my wheelchair.

"The doors and ramp do operate on electricity and also with hydraulic pumps," I said.

"How do you drive this thing? You can't use the brake and gas pedal with your feet." She peered into the dim cavern at the back of the van.

"Hop in the passenger side and I'll meet you up front." I pushed my wheels onto the ramp and flipped the toggle switch to lift me up level to the van's floor.

After I showed her the hand controls and the "suicide knob" on the steering wheel that I used for turning corners, she leaned over and pecked me on the cheek.

"I sure had fun tonight." She smiled and slid back to the passenger seat and hopped down to let Mom get in. "Here, Beverly, I'll give you a boost."

Then she wished us good night and ambled back toward her parents' front porch. As I backed out of the driveway, she turned and lingered, giving me an unassuming wave of her hand.

Mom was chatty on the drive home.

"You and Josephine sure seemed to hit it off tonight," she began. The inquisition followed.

"Do you think you'll ask her out? I'm sure she'll say yes. Did you find out what kind of work she does? Why does she live with Herb and Betty? Has she ever been married? Engaged? How old do you think she is? I think she's a very nice girl, Will. I just want you to be happy, to find a nice girl and get married. Do you think she's marriage material?"

Relief flooded in when she stepped out of my van and headed toward her front door. Mom was spot-on, though. The following weeks bloomed into a full-on romance for Josephine and me.

She wasn't exactly the hot pants that Sheila was, but she wasn't a dog either. Josephine was sexy in her own way. She wasn't petite. She dominated a room when she walked in, solidly built and tall—at least six feet, which would have suited me well since I was six-foot-two. Her ample breasts spilled out of every blouse she wore—a plus in my book.

Later in our dating, when we were fully established as a couple, she took to leaning over me in my wheelchair and nestling my head between them, caressing my chin with her soft hands.

"No fair!" I'd exclaim. "Come 'round front so I can *really* enjoy those jugs!" She accommodated my command every time.

Since the night we met, I dreamed about those big breasts. I was going to take pleasure in them if it was the last thing on earth I ever did. I found out, however, that Josephine was not a pushover. Dinner and movie dates were about as far as she went for quite a while.

Proud as I was about learning techniques for making out with girls while in a wheelchair, I got nervous around Josephine. Sure, she'd wrap her arms around me and sit in my lap to smooch, but as soon as my hand wandered south to graze one of her abundant breasts, she'd squirm out of reach and jump up, claiming she needed to refresh her drink, or had to go to the "little girls' room." I had to take another approach to earn her trust. How could I convince her that we could have a normal — and exclusive — relationship? I decided to let her know how I felt and that I wanted to deepen our bond.

On a warm June evening, I took her to a game over in Tempe. The Sun Devils were playing at the Packard Stadium, my favorite field baseball since I could get a great spot for my wheelchair. I held her hand and made sure that she was comfortable. I showered her with all the suaveness I could muster, and it seemed to pay off. She kept leaning over and kissing my cheek, whispering how much fun she was having and that she was glad she was my girlfriend.

But that didn't tell me what her temperature was when it came to a full commitment. I tried to ease into the subject.

"I really had a great time tonight. And they slaughtered the opposition — those Sun Devils could end up as the PAC-12 Champions this year!"

"Yeah, it *was* fun tonight. Hey, do you want to stop at Romano's on North Tatum?" Josephine asked. "It's on the way home and I could go for a nice drink that's not draft beer."

"We could, no problem. Let's grab some grub too. I'm kind of hungry. I can't eat those ballpark dogs, and it *is* past my dinnertime!"

As soon as we were seated at our table, I ordered Josephine a glass of house wine, remembering her aversion to draft beer.

"Thanks, Will! You must have read my mind." Josephine's blue eyes sparkled at me as she bustled with her purse and settled into her chair.

"Sure thing, babe. Now—heh, heh, heh—can you read *my* mind?" I winked and pushed my glasses up on my nose.

"Yes, I can—and you need to get it out of the gutter." She glared at me, but her off-center smile negated her stern reply.

"You can rest assured it's not in the gutter. In fact, I wanted to talk to you about something, well, pretty important."

The waiter interrupted with bread and olive oil, and Josephine ordered another glass of wine. A few minutes later, I'd barely finished my first beer when she ordered a third drink. This threw me off course.

"You're pretty thirsty. What gives?" I wanted to show care and concern, but alarm seeped into my voice.

"Don't preach to me, William Walter! I've had a tough week at work and I need to 'wine down' as they say." We laughed then, and because we were both starving, I chalked it up to that and her need to de-stress.

The conversation hadn't gone as planned, though, and we left Romano's, Josephine a bit tipsy and me with a full belly and lingering questions.

A few weeks later, I got my answer—in a big way. We'd been out on our standard Friday night date, dinner and a movie. We were parked in front of her parents' house, debating the merits of the movie *Pretty Woman*. I'd opted for that one instead of *Red October* to try to get Josephine in a romantic mood. But Josephine swung the other way on the pendulum, saying she hated the whole premise of the story.

"Besides," she said, "prostitutes in real life don't look like Julia Richards, and they don't get breaks like that, either!"

"You're right—it was unrealistic," I said, wanting to be agreeable, but longing to take the conversation in another direction. "But it was just a movie—besides, they had fun together."

"Yeah, what girl wouldn't want Richard Gere to swoop in and knock her off her feet?" Josephine snorted and huffed a little but had a faraway look in her eyes.

I was wound up tight by then, wondering what her feelings were for me and what kind of future—if any—we might have together. I decided to broach the subject of our relationship.

"Josephine," I started slowly, pacing my words. "You know you mean the world to me."

"Sure, Will." She seemed to drill into my head, reading my thoughts. She made it easy by saying it first. "I love you, sweetie, with all my heart."

I could hardly believe my ears. She loves me! "I—I

love you too."

"So, what's stopping us? Let's get hitched!"

I couldn't have said it any better.

Ecstatic one minute, I panicked the next. One concern gnawed at me, one that I'd battled with a lot. I had to ask the question to be confident that this relationship could last.

"Now wait just a minute, babe. I think you just pro-posed to me—it should be the other way around," I said. "And I do want to marry you, believe me, it's what I want more than anything else."

"I hear a 'but' in what you're saying," Josephine said. "Should I be worried?"

"I have to ask you something really important."

"Okay, shoot. You know we can talk about anything at all."

I'd spent weeks at the computer, searching the Internet for information about men who have suffered an SCI and who struggle to maintain an erection or who can't even get an erection because the pathways between the brain and penis don't function properly.

The brain stimulates specific neuronal pathways that will connect with the penis via the spinal cord, to pro-duce an increased blood flow to the penis, causing it to become erect. As a previous normal male, I knew that I'd get boners just by seeing, hearing, or fantasizing about erotic things—physical stimulation wasn't a necessity. Because my spinal cord was severed completely, there was no way to get the message from my brain to my "second brain" below my belt.

"Yeah, I know that. Well, truthfully, I'm worried about sex."

Josephine threw back her head, in hysterics. She slapped her leg, then punched me in the arm.

"You big goofball—don't you know I've already thought about that? I read up on quadriplegics and found out that some paralyzed men can still get an erection. But more important than that, Will—people have sex in all sorts of different ways. You've got to be creative about it, but that's half the fun."

"Well, I guess I do get reflex erections sometimes, like when my catheter gets hooked up. But I can't imagine that lasting long enough to be satisfying from a woman's point of view. I just don't want to disappoint you in that department."

Josephine slipped out of the car seat and sat on my lap.

"Honey, I'm willing to see this as an exciting journey to find other ways to satisfy each other. Remember, I have a part in this too."

"Sure, but it's the man's job to make his woman happy, in every way."

"Well, what about oral sex? That works for me."

Wow! Was I really hearing this right? She was suggesting something that I'd only had a real experience with a few times before my accident.

"And your brain isn't numb. I bet if I kissed your ear-lobe and your neck, you'd enjoy it."

In a few months, we were married. I was a happy man. We were well on our way to realizing the dream I'd carried for nearly fifteen years. The goals I'd written down several years ago in a college paper were material-izing. I was going to retire at age fifty, own a large ranch in Colorado, grow and smoke quality pot, and take care of my wife and children.

Josephine was eager to learn about my daily care and routines. We had a home-care nurse come in to train her on the basics, and Mom still came by to show her some of the tricks we'd learned over the years for transferring me.

"Can you stay for dinner, Bev?" Josephine asked on one of Mom's first visits.

"Yeah, we've got plenty of food," I chimed in, even though I knew it wouldn't take much convincing.

"I'll stay only on one condition," Mom said.

"What's that?" A trace of panic in Josephine's reply told me she was nervous about making a good impres-sion on her new mother-in-law.

"Call me 'Mom'—that is, if you're comfortable with that."

"No problem—will do!" Josephine's face glowed. The bonding had begun.

We'd get to playing cards after dinner, or a Yahtzee game or two. I'd already learned that Josephine was as competitive as I was, so the verbal sparring would start up. She'd yell and jab her fist at me if she won. I'd bristle back at her, then we'd all crack up. It was good to hear so much laughter in the house. I'd forgotten how comfortable things could be with someone to love and be loved back.

One night, after Mom left and we were putting the game board away, I noticed a high school yearbook of Josephine's under the stack of games on the coffee table.

"Hey, what's this—your senior yearbook?" I was more than curious, because Josephine hadn't shared much with me about her younger years. "Can I take a look at it?"

"Sure!" Josephine sat down on the sofa beside me and pulled the book onto her lap. The cover showed a milquetoast school in the Midwest: Eden Prairie High School's 1968 Yearbook. The photos could have been from my own yearbook, filled with shots of students on stage during school plays, football and basketball action, photos of kids with the same hairdos, the same goofy smiles—but unfamiliar faces.

We got to laughing then, because it seemed like every photo of Josephine showed her gazing at something off camera—spaced out was the term I used.

Josephine giggled, saying most likely she was just stoned. There was a lot of pot-smoking in those days, she said—usually at lunchtime; then they'd go back to class for English Lit, where the ink flowed and flowery poems bloomed on the paper.

"I tried to convince myself that pot was my drug of choice," she said. "But it was alcohol that I truly loved. I even threw a kegger our last day of school. My friend Cleve drove me to the Southside bar outside of town to score the keg, loaded it into his blue VW Bug, and jammed out to Staring Lake. Middle of the afternoon, since all of us seniors got out early that last day."

"There was lots of beer-drinking in my circle of friends too," I confessed. "But my senior party was a dry one. You know, I was already in the chair then. I think I popped open a can or two, just to toast with the boys. But I went home pretty early that night. Mom had to work the next day, and she had to get me to bed. I didn't want to worry her."

"God, I didn't even *think* about that," Josephine told me. "I'm sorry, Will."

"No big deal. Hey, let's crack open that ice cream that's in the freezer."

In the following months, we fell into a schedule that worked great for both of us. Since Josephine didn't have to be at work until nine, she'd help me with my morning hygiene, get me dressed and fed, then walk me to the van with chatter about her upcoming day. She loved the work itself—criminal litigation cases—but her comments about her impossibly arrogant and ignorant boss (the attorney) gave away her frustrations. She hated working for the jerk, but she felt stuck since we needed the income. I'd try cracking a joke to make her laugh, get her in a good mood for the day.

We always kissed and I'd hold her tight for a long minute before punching the "up" button on the lift. She'd wait in the driveway and watch as I backed out, throwing me a kiss before I turned and drove away. After nearly twenty years as a wheelchair-bound bachelor, life took a turn for the better. I loved being married, and to such a sweet woman.

She did, however, have her share of quirks. Josephine was obsessed with exercising, claiming that she had to hammer on it all the time just so she could keep her weight at an acceptable level. She'd hit the gym and do workouts for nearly three hours at a stretch. Or she'd call up her friend Rhiannon and they'd take their ten-speeds and ride down toward Scottsdale, a route that took them on an ambitious forty-mile round trip.

I'd get lonely sometimes when she was gone like that, but she made up for it by cooking delicious meals. She'd learned a lot from her mother, and we never lacked for hearty dinners. When it wasn't too hot outside, we'd sit out on the patio for a while before our meal, and Josephine would expertly pop the cork on a crisp, cool white wine, claiming that it would pair well with the menu she had in mind. We'd toast, congratulating ourselves on a day well done, and admire the blooming desert plants near the patio. Sometimes, she seemed to spend an inordinate amount of time dashing into the house to check on the food, but at the time it didn't seem odd to me. I just chalked it up to her meticulous attention to recipes.

With all of this normalcy on the surface, I couldn't imagine that anything could be less than perfect. I'd ignored the signs in the beginning, thinking that Josephine's drinking was due to the hassles from her job, or running around doing things for her parents, or helping take care of me and the house chores on top of working full time. She was really good at rationalizing her behavior too. Even my counselor training didn't help me to see through it.

"I drink because I enjoy it. I have no problem *not* drinking when I need to. Remember when my doctor had me on that five days of antibiotics? I didn't have a drop then." If I questioned her about it, she'd always have a logical comeback.

It happened a lot of times when we were on our way to her parents' house for dinner and she'd insist we stop off at the liquor store for another bottle.

"Isn't a bottle of wine for the four of us enough, honey?" Even I could hear the desperate hope in my voice. "I know it's healthy to have a glass of wine a day, I'm okay with that. But I'm worried about you, Josephine."

"Here's my gripe about that one-drink-a-day rule. For me, alcohol isn't medicine to be taken in measured doses. It's more about my psyche. That first sip smoothes out the edges of a rough day."

"I get it. We all need to unwind after a long day at work."

"Besides that, it's a ritual. I love having a glass of chardonnay while cooking dinner and chatting with you. Then there's the importance of alcohol to my social life. Almost every event I go to that's work-related is at one of those new wine bars popping up everywhere. So, I just divvy up my seven-drink total weekly allotment into those few days when I can have three or four, and then spread the others out during the week."

I couldn't argue with that, especially since she always got up and went to work and seemed to be keeping it together for the most part. On the outside, things were normal for us; we worked during the day, Josephine would cook dinner, and we'd watch some TV at night. On the weekends, it was baseball games or dinner with the parents or browsing the flea markets.

Then we made a major shift. I was making good money at the Arizona Bridge for Independent Living (ABIL), and we started talking about how great it would be if Josephine could step away from her stressful and demanding career to be at home. She was excited by the idea, and listed all the things she was going to do to get the house and yard back in shape. She wanted to grow a garden and get a dog. She wanted to write a book and play the guitar again.

I was all for it—maybe this was the answer to her issues with the alcohol. I'd noticed that she spent a lot of time running out to the garage in the evenings, and several times I'd found empties stashed in the clothes hamper. I refused to face the possibility that she could be an alcoholic. So I went along with the plan.

Little did I know that my wife was headed for the depths of despair. Within a few short months, she'd nearly destroyed herself. She hardly cooked anymore and seemed only interested in sharing "happy hour" drinks with me as soon as I wheeled in the door at night. She'd tell me about all the things she'd done all day, how busy she'd been, but I didn't see the results. She'd seem a little tipsy, maybe slurring a few words or stumble around a few times, but I didn't know that by our first drink together at night, she was already two bottles down and starting her third.

"Come on, Will. Let's sit on the patio and relax after a hard day," she'd say.

"What about the garden?" I asked. "Don't you still want to plant one?"

She wanted to till up the corner of the yard in April and plant soon after in May. It was now the middle of June and still not a spade of dirt had been turned. Instead of the backyard oasis we talked about creating, the grass withered from lack of water and the patio gathered rubbish and a jumble of cast-offs from garage sales that Josephine scoured almost on a daily basis. We did adopt a puppy, a sweet little mutt. But the puppy just added to the mess, tearing up stuff from the patio and strewing it all over the yard.

Josephine's antics were sometimes comical, but

many times embarrassing. The puppy—she named him Amos—was an escape artist that gave Josephine no end to her frustrations. Not only would he dart out as soon as she opened the front door to a guest calling, but he'd race down the street hot on the scent of a cat or squirrel. She was out of it one evening when Amos escaped. I figured she'd been sipping wine since mid-afternoon. She got mad and jumped on her bike to run him down and lasso him with some rope. I didn't ask what happened when they got back.

"That dammed dog! He did it again," she sputtered. "He was after some critter under a pile of branches in Bob's yard. I had to crawl in after him and drag him out by his hind legs." Her flushed face and fiery eyes silenced any comment from me. The pup was clutched under her arm, squirming but squished too tight to free himself.

Amos didn't like Josephine. She'd call for him and he'd tuck his tail, his ears lowered and eyebrows raised. He'd slink over to her, head hanging, sit in front of her but looking past her. She'd rough him up, tossing his head back and forth between her hands, and slapping him hard on his back.

"Oh, you're a good dog, Amos," she'd say. He'd scram away from her and come to me, trying to hide underneath the wheelchair.

I started noticing other dogs didn't really take to Josephine either. They'd avoid her if they could even if she was coaxing them to come to her or petting them.

That should have been a red flag for me. When animals, especially dogs, have this kind of behavior around a human, there's something out of kilter with the human.

Amos started peeing whenever Josephine walked into the room. He started howling when we put him outside in the yard, and ripping up anything that wasn't nailed down.

Other things went downhill too.

"Why aren't you and Rhiannon riding together?" I asked. The bike rides had diminished; she'd drag herself off to the gym a few times a week now, and always seemed too tired to go anywhere on the weekends.

"She downright pisses me off," said Josephine. "She doesn't work in the summer and then acts like I have all the time in the world too."

"But you seemed to find the time before, last fall and winter. What's changed?" I asked, trying to draw her out and maybe get her enthused about doing something healthy again.

Josephine glared at me. "She tells people that we took first place at the Mount Lemmon race last year."

Raising her voice, she added, "First of all, we haven't raced for three years, and this is old news that no one cares about. Second, we never took first place—the best we ever did was third place!

I let it drop—I'd never heard Josephine talk like that about her best friend before. Something bigger was going on with her.

She got pissed off at me too. She was doing a crappy job with my hygiene and personal care, and when I'd bring up the subject, she'd erupt.

"Joey, you know I have to start eating dinner early. It's almost seven and you haven't even started cooking yet."

"You're just so dammed picky," she'd scream. "Who cares if we eat by five fucking o'clock? Only old people do that, for Christ's sake!"

"But you know that I have to have a couple of hours to digest my food before getting ready for bed."

"All right, fine!" She'd stomp into the kitchen, mumbling to herself. Once in a while, I'd catch a "fucking" this or "shit head" that as she slammed pots onto the stove or flung open drawers, utensils clanging out the discord that filled our house.

The deterioration was insidious, incremental—so much so that I didn't realize how bad things were getting. It was early summer and the bands were starting to play outdoors at the parks again. We'd decided to run on down to Cave Creek Park on Thunderbird to check it out on a Friday night. We were doing okay, sitting at a bistro table, Josephine with her never-empty glass of wine and me with some iced tea (I had to drive, as usual). The music was decent and we were flirting with each other and joking about the weirdos in the crowd. *Maybe tonight would be somewhat normal.* But as soon as the MC announced the main band, Josephine jumped up and melted into the crowd. I assumed she wanted to worm her way into the mash of bodies in front of the stage to catch the first few songs, something she did regularly, so I wasn't alarmed at first. Then she didn't come back to the table. There was a ruckus in front of the stage. The crowd parted as if they were grass laid down by a stiff wind. The paramedics ran in with a stretcher, swallowed momentarily by the mass of bodies. When they emerged from the throng, I saw the royal purple blouse. Josephine's favorite. Oh, God. Here we go.

I wheeled out to my van, noting the ambulance name and knowing they were headed to the hospital out on Van Buren Road. I brought Josephine home that night, after the ER nurses pumped her with fluids and anti-nausea medicine. She was still so out of it, all the way home she kept mumbling, "I'm sorry, Will. I'm so sorry. I don't ever want to drink again." I heard her words but didn't believe her. She'd made those promises before and no more than a day later, she'd be cracking open a bottle and singing the same old tune.

Josephine surprised me this time, though. The next morning, while she was getting me out of bed (with a few trips to the bathroom to pray to the porcelain god), she said she knew someone at work who was in "AA," the Alcoholics Anonymous program. She was going to ask her for help.

"You know I'm behind you on this a hundred per-cent," I told her. "Anything I can do to help, I will. Joey,

I want you to be happy, to be my wife, to be the person I married."

"I know. I'm serious this time—I need to stop drinking, but I just don't think I can. I've tried so many times and something drives me back to it every time. I'm—I'm really scared, babe. I'm terrified to stop and terrified to keep drinking."

She sat on my lap and wrapped her arms around me, sobbing into my shoulder. I could almost hear both our hearts breaking.

She went to her first AA meeting that night. She'd called one of her co-workers that morning, someone she knew who was in the program. Paula told her, "That's great Josephine! There's a meeting tonight at seven over at the church on Payson Street. I'll pick you up at 6:30. But call me before that if you feel like you're going to drink."

"Oh, don't worry about that. I'm really sick with this hangover today. I'm just going to rest. And, Paula — thanks for doing this."

That was the start of a pretty good time for Josephine and me. She stayed sober for three or four weeks, going to meetings and studying their "Big Book" as they called it.

Then, one night she came home after a meeting with a brown bag and two bottles of wine, claiming that the "AA thing" wasn't working for her.

By the end of summer, the house fell into a filthy mess, dirty dishes stacked high, laundry piled in the corners. Josephine took to lounging on the sofa, smoking cigarettes and talking on the phone for hours on end. She still did our morning and evening routines for my care, but dinner was hit or miss. Sometimes she'd pass out on the couch right after the 5:30 news, so I'd get back in the van and hit a drive-through somewhere down on Camelback, hoping that by the time I got back home, she'd be revived enough to help me get to bed.

My only relief was my job at ABIL as a counselor. At least there, I was in my element—working with other guys who were disabled, some like me in wheelchairs, blind, or with any number of conditions that incapacitated them.

I kept up a cool front, showing them what a great role model I was with my master's degree and full-time career, marriage, owning my home and driving my own van. But I hated going home at night, not knowing what I'd find.

I was puttering on the computer one evening and could hear some hissing noises in the kitchen. I assumed Josephine was cooking. I was hungry and hollered to her, "Hey, honey! I'm starved—what's for dinner?" She didn't answer. Then I smelled hot oil, and as I rolled into the hallway, a brown haze billowed out of the kitchen.

I backed into the den and grabbed the phone.

"Mom! You have to get here *quick*—I think Josephine is trying to burn the house down—*please*, come over as fast as you can." I made my way back down the hall and turned in to the kitchen. Josephine was nowhere in sight; the oil in the frying pan was seconds away from bursting into flames. I wheeled as close as I dared and shoved the pan off the burner, then backed out of the kitchen as fast as my deformed hands could grasp the knobs on my wheels. The adrenaline was pumping now; as I reeled back into the dim living room, I made out Josephine's lumpy shape on the sofa. She was passed out, I was sure of that.

"Josephine! Wake up!" I thrust my fist into her arm, trying to rouse her.

Finally, she turned toward me, sluggish and bleary-eyed.

"What the *HELL* are you doing in here sleeping?! The stove almost caught fire just now!"

"Sorry, Will. I was so tired, I just wanted to rest a minute. I forgot I had turned the flame on under the pan." It wasn't just her hangdog look, but the casual way she brushed it off that infuriated me.

"*Christ*, Josephine! A house fire is the *LAST* thing we need right now!"

"I know, I know." She fell back into the sofa, pulling the blanket over her face. A muffled "Sorry" drifted from the shadows.

I spun around and headed to the den, ready to explode again. I couldn't think straight—I should have called 9-1-1 for the fire department—for all I knew, the kitchen was burning by now.

Mom showed up a few minutes later, opening the doors and windows to flush the smoke from the house. She went to check on Josephine. She couldn't budge her; Josephine was out cold. Mom said she was still breathing, but she was scared that something was really wrong with her.

"Yeah, there is—she's stone-cold drunk!" I yelled, then felt sorry that my aggravation was coming out sideways at Mom.

"I think we should call the ambulance," Mom countered with her usual common sense.

"Maybe, I don't know. Let's call Herb and Betty first. I think they should come and get her. Mom, I don't think I can let her stay here anymore." I felt tears welling up. "I don't feel safe with her, and I don't know what to do to help her." I hesitated; found the courage to go on. "I've—I've tried everything, and it doesn't seem to change things."

"I know you have, Will." Mom embraced me, then looked me square in the face. "I just want you two to be happy."

Twenty minutes later, Josephine's parents were at the door. Betty went to the bedroom to root out some clothes for Josephine and tossed them into an old ratty suitcase she found under the bed. Herb scooped Josephine up off the sofa, holding her up as they both stumbled out to the car. Betty appeared from Josephine's bedroom and leaned over me, her tear-streaked cheeks pressing into my own.

"We love you, Will. Herb and I—well, we've done this before. We'll take Josephine home with us. We can take care of her until she's feeling better."

I watched them pull out of the driveway. My chest hurt. I knew it wasn't the smoke—it was my broken heart. I had no idea when I'd next see my wife.

BEVERLY: SPRING TRAINING

*Love is the most important thing in
the world, but baseball is pretty good too.*

— Yogi Berra

When we first moved to Phoenix, Will and I got interested in the baseball teams running their spring trainings here, and we spent many Saturdays following the Cactus League. We discovered which stadiums were set up best for his wheelchair, those that offered the easiest access and that let us watch from advantageous spots in the stands.

This was our usual weekly outing for three or four years, and we both enjoyed it immensely. Then I became "second fiddle" to Will's new girlfriend, Josephine. I didn't blame her, or him. It just happened naturally, but also due to the fact that I somewhat tried to help with the matchmaking process. My friends Herb and Betty had been square dancing with the Sunny Slope group, the same one I went to, for over a year. One night, we decided to get together for dinner and introduce our children. Their daughter Josephine was single and close to Will's age, so we thought it would do no harm to get everyone together.

They invited us to dinner, and that was the start of it all. Before long, I was no longer Will's date for the baseball games. But I didn't mind. As long as my son was happy, as long as he was experiencing a love life that anyone should be able to enjoy, I was happy about it.

Things progressed with them, and several months later, they announced their impending wedding. I was thrilled! At last, my son, who had always wanted a life partner, despite the obstacles that his condition presented him with, was realizing his dream.

I really loved Josephine. She was a smart woman, independent and strong. She reminded me a lot of myself at a younger age. I could see that she adored Will, that she was fascinated with his sense of adventure and romantic way with women.

She also took over the majority of Will's daily care, and for the first time in two decades, I was free to live my life as I wanted. I started traveling with my little sister. She'd fly out from Wisconsin and we'd take off for the West Coast, or whatever destination suited us at the time.

I admired Josephine for committing her love to a man who was disabled, that she could look past his limitations and accept him for the bright soul he was. I always said we cannot pick the package that our love is delivered to us in. She proved that point quite well.

The kids were really happy for a few years. Then I noticed a deterioration of sorts. The yard sank into a neglected patch of dried grass; yard sale junk piled up in the garage and spilled into the breezeway. The house was cluttered and dusty, which wasn't at all the case when Josephine first moved in with Will.

Then, one evening, I got a panicked call from Will and I heard the fright in his voice. He was yelling into the phone that Josephine was passed out on the sofa and the house was burning down. I told him to call 9-1-1 and drove over as fast as I could.

When I got there, I ran in the front door and found the smoking frying pan on the stove, but no fire. I called for Will and heard him answer from the back. He was already sitting in the breezeway for fresh air, so I rushed back in, opening windows to flush the smoke out and looking for Josephine. She was out cold on the sofa. I could tell she was breathing, but I couldn't rouse her to get her out of the house. I told Will that we're calling the ambulance. He said, no, to call Herb and Betty first, so I finally gave in and called them instead.

They arrived soon after and gathered their daughter up, rousing her from her stupor and escorting her between them to the car.

Betty told me they'd been through this before, that

she'd had "episodes" of relapse with her drinking. I saw the worry in Betty's face and told her I would help with anything at all. She just shook her head, saying they'd been through it several times before, and thanked me for helping their daughter.

Will and I watched from the front yard as they drove away. I put my arm around my son.

"You've done the best you can, Will. It's up to Josephine now to figure out what to do to help herself. It's out of your hands, son."

"I know, Mom," he said. "But it still hurts like hell."

I kept in touch with Betty over the next weeks to check on Josephine's condition. Those weeks stretched into months and I finally realized she was never going back to Will. She was just too ill to be able to re-enter a normal life. I dreaded the thought of the aftereffect on Will, what a blow it would be for him. At the same time, I ached for Josephine's suffering. They were meant for each other. But a powerful, insidious disease held them apart like boxing opponents in separate corners of the ring. I knew that they would never overcome this formidable beast.

WILL: CLOSE CALL

Man can live about forty days without food,
about three days without water, about eight minutes without air,
but only for one second without hope.

— Charles Darwin

I hadn't seen Josephine since her parents took her from my house that night. I found out later, talking to Betty on the phone, that they'd taken her to the emergency room. The ER doctor suspected that not only was she at a toxic level of alcohol poisoning, but she also showed signs of some type of opiate ingestion. I'd filled a prescription for Vicodin a few days before for the massive headaches I'd been getting. Josephine knew about every pill I swallowed, and she could get them any time without me noticing it. She was the dispenser, the nurse, the keeper of the coveted substances. I hadn't dreamed that she could have cross-addictions too.

Betty was hysterical telling me about that horrid night. They didn't pump Josephine's stomach like they'd done before during these awful episodes; instead, the ER doctor had given her activated charcoal, a method not used often.

"The doctor told me that he suspected Josephine had ingested other substances, some sort of painkillers. He said he was going to give her activated charcoal to try to absorb the toxins in her system." From Betty's testimony about that night, I learned that the doctor finally decided not to order dialysis, an extreme measure for treating alcohol poisoning.

He told Betty, "That's only done when patients have impaired hepatic functions and dialysis is the best avenue for clearing an ethanol load." I knew Josephine had been out of it, but I had no idea she was that far gone. I felt like a pile of dog crap, thinking I was the cause of her troubles that night.

When the hospital staff finally allowed her parents into the ER room, Josephine tried to look at them, head lolling about and eyes out of focus. Disheveled and tangled, her beautiful blonde hair hung about her face, and the remnants of charcoal-loaded vomit around her mouth gave her a ghoulish appearance.

"She vus a mess." Betty choked out the words, sobbing into the phone. "But she iss better now. Don't worry; she will be fine at home now."

I knew she *wouldn't* be fine. The disease had her in

its grasp, tight as a pit bull's jaw locked onto a child's throat. She was defenseless against alcohol's grip. I was convinced that she would spiral downward even more. I *thought* she'd hit bottom with the stove incident. Time after demoralizing time, the incidents had come more frequently. Each time, her capacity to function normally had ebbed away. Sweet, soppy, full of transparent excuses, my wife crumbled before my eyes. We all waited hopefully, her parents and me, wringing our hands and whispering that *maybe this* time, things will be different. *Maybe* she will be able to get some help from someone or something more powerful, more knowledgeable than us.

After one of her "episodes," for a week or two, she'd go to AA meetings, full of good intentions and ready to face her addiction head-on. I'd be full of hope, wanting her to be the happy-go-lucky girl I'd met a year ago. The next week, her drunken antics repulsed me, infuriated me, and scared the shit out of me. I'd worked with disabled guys for years, building a support system for them, giving them an outlet for their frustrations and ways to work around the obstacles. Why couldn't Josephine do the same with her AA group? I couldn't figure out why it was so impossible for her to take hold of the simple ideas that those AA people were trying to teach her.

When I saw that she couldn't stay sober, even while she was going to meetings and calling her sponsor all the time, I gave up. I decided, *If you can't beat 'em, join 'em.* That's when I started drinking pretty heavily. It helped blot out the pain—sometimes—of watching her stumble around the house at night, trying to maintain some kind of normal home life.

Earlier in the day before the stove incident happened, I'd been given a bottle of Dewar's 12 blended scotch whiskey at work, a holiday gift. It packed a potent 80 percent ABV rating—smooth going down the gullet, but it hit you like a runaway train. I realized too late that it was a mistake to show it to Josephine, suggesting that we have a snort before dinner. She'd proceeded to not only snort a few, but to literally guzzle the contents in a matter of less than an hour.

I blamed myself for the miserable results of our short-lived holiday celebration. Why didn't I just leave that bottle in the van that night? Why did I make it so easy for her to fall over the edge, to drown in her alcohol fixation, and me without lifting a finger to resist?

Weeks later, downhearted and beating myself up over these glum thoughts, I couldn't sleep at night and dozed off at work during group sessions. Work was a muddle of days, one tangled into another and without benchmark or recall.

I told my boss, "It would be better if I wasn't here." He told me things would get better, and coming to work would help more than sitting at home, staring at the walls. Besides, Mom was there every morning, waking me up and dragging me through our daily care routine. She tried to pull me out of my slump, saying that we should go to a ball game or out to dinner. I couldn't bring myself to go out. I'd panic at the thought of leaving the house for anything else besides my job.

I started asking Mom about Dad's accident, and I wanted to find out the truth about his brother Edwin—the fifth uncle. My obsession with their deaths alarmed my mom.

"I just want to understand what happened to them," I told her. "And how were you able to get through things after Dad was gone—raising us three boys by yourself? What kept you going?"

We'd have long discussions then, about never giving up and how there is always something or someone to give us hope. I still felt hopeless, helpless, and worthless. Other times, unexpected rage would overwhelm me and I'd strike out at Mom, landing sideways blows to her self-esteem too.

"Why the hell did you go and do that for?" I screamed at her one day, when she had accidentally put my favorite drinking cup on a higher shelf in the cupboard, too high for me to reach by myself.

"Son, settle down, please! I'll get the cup down for you." She shook her head and muttered something too faint for me to hear. I knew I'd hurt her feelings—she wasn't normally one to grumble about anything.

The weeks dragged out. I endured the mechanical motions of advertising and interviewing for Josephine's replacement—that is, a home health care worker. After plowing through a few dozen applicants, I settled on one who seemed the least offensive and the most normal of the menagerie that had paraded into my home for interviews. I really didn't care one way or another if they were nut cases or not. I just wanted to relieve Mom of her nursing duties. My indifferent decision resulted in hiring Dana. She wasn't due to start for a couple of weeks, which was fine by me.

I wanted a little more time to myself before a stranger began living in my house again. I had some things to take care of before—before my final plan was put in motion. Life had finally got me down. I hated myself. I'd failed miserably as a husband. Why go on living with all this gut wrenching guilt? I needed to release all my pent-up remorse and just bleed out.

I started getting all my life insurance policies in order, making sure that Mom was the beneficiary. I ran red lights on the way to work, shaking my gnarled fist at the other drivers who had to swerve out of my way. I called my cousin Gage one night and told him how much I appreciated the times he'd taken me out on the town. I called Gordy and told him that if anything ever happened to me, he could take my van and sell it.

I set out for Sedona on a Saturday morning, telling Mom I just needed to get out of town for the day, hit the open road and clear my head. I'd waited until this particular Saturday, because I knew she had accounts to call on for month-end accounting stuff and she wouldn't be able to come with me.

"I'm not sure that's a great idea, taking off by your-self," she said as she hauled me from the bathroom in the hydraulic sling machine. "Why don't you call one of the boys? I'll bet Gage or your brother would like to go with you."

"Naw, I don't want to bother with trying to wake one of them up early—they always go out on Friday nights. It's no big deal, Mom. I'll call you."

"What's so important that you have to go to Sedona, anyway?" Her eyes bored into me.

I turned my chair away before she could see the lie in my eyes. "Well, I've been reading about those spiritual vortexes and how those are supposed to help you heal. I just thought it might do me some good, help me get over this Josephine thing."

I knew she wouldn't argue with my logic on that top-ic. She turned to leave, and then turned back, making me promise to call when I got back home.

"I can come back over and help you to bed," she said.

"That's okay, Mom. I'll call Gordy and he'll come over when I get home—it'll be late, and he'll be up partying anyway. He can crash here and get me up in the morning too. Give you a break for the weekend."

It was late November, but it was still warm and sun-ny. I had Mom throw my light jacket into the van when she left the house, and asked her to fill my sixty-four-ounce mug that I kept propped on the engine cover.

In twenty minutes, I was cruising north on I-17 out of Phoenix proper.

I chuckled, thinking about my excuse of going to a spiritual vortex. A few years earlier, some "New Age" writer touted the concept of a harmonic convergence. According to him, during two specific days in August 1987, the earth would slip out of its "time beam" and spin off into space. Only by the psychic efforts of the human race would Earth remain where it was supposed to be. He wanted people to gather at sacred places around the globe and focus their energies to keep the earth safe and thus escort in a new era of harmony and love. He claimed that Sedona was a sacred place, so why not gather there. Of course, the earth didn't slip away and twirl uncontrollably. The convergence worked!

"Ha!" I thought of the real reason I wanted to find a vortex. I wanted to find one that would suck me into oblivion just like water swirling down the drain in a bathtub. Or a desert dust devil to come pick me up and carry me away to unconsciousness.

A couple of hours later, I pulled into Sedona, scouting for a fast-food drive-through. Not an easy task, since almost every commercial outlet was camouflaged behind huge desert shrubs. I had to drive all the way out to West Sedona, six miles out, before uncovering a Burger King on Highway 89. I asked the cashier at the window about the vortexes, and how I might find them. She said the Red Rock Visitor's Center at the corner of Big Sandy and the highway a few blocks down would have maps. She added that I'd have to buy a park pass for five dollars.

"Thanks, I'll check it out. Keep the change." I drove away from the window and pulled into a parking spot. After wolfing down my lunch, I headed in the direction she'd pointed. When I wheeled into the center, the clerk behind the desk greeted me with a gusto in his voice that belied a salesman's goal. After chitchatting about where I was from, what I was looking to do in Sedona, and drawing several lines and arrows on a map that he boasted was not to scale, he gave the pitch.

"I can get you free tickets to see the live international jazz show, with Kaja Rollo performing, tonight at the Sound Bites Grill."

"I'm not interested. I'm just here to get my park pass and a map."

"You seem like a well-to-do man that would like a great getaway place. The Hilton is showing their exclusive condos from two to four today; if you go, I can give you these show tickets right now."

"Really, I'm not into buying a condo and I won't have time to go to the jazz show tonight."

"The Hilton does have handicapped accessible units for the same price as their regular ones." He acted like he hadn't heard a word I said.

"No, thanks. I just need a park pass. Here's my five dollars."

"Oh, the girl that sells those isn't here today. You can

go to a Circle K or Basha's grocery store to get one."

"You can't sell me a park pass?"

"No, sorry. The clerk has today off. She'll be in tomorrow if you want to come back then."

This disgusting little gnat was really annoying me now. I turned my chair and headed to the door. If I could have slammed it on my way out, I would have. Screw it. *If they bust me for not having a pass, so be it.* At least I had the map and could find my way to one of the vortex areas. I found a city park and pulled over to study the map; after looking it over, I picked Airport Mesa. I knew I wouldn't be able to actually *get* to the vortex, but the view from the airport would give me some panoramic views of Sedona's best-known red rock landmarks. Later in the day, it would be deserted too. Planes didn't land or take off after the sun went down, so I figured I'd be pretty much alone up there in an hour or so. It was late November, so the tourists had thinned out considerably, and plane traffic had dropped off next to nothing. I wanted isolation, a place where I couldn't be found unless I wanted to be found.

I pulled the van up near the tarmac at sunset. From my vantage point, I picked out Courthouse Butte and Bell Rock to the south. Cathedral Rock blazed orange a bit further west of Bell Rock. I turned my gaze northwest and spotted Chimney Rock. Check. The map may not have been to scale, but it was good enough for me to settle myself in for the night. Normal methods weren't going to work. I couldn't jump off the top of Cathedral Rock. I couldn't jump out of a plane or throw myself in front of a train. Using a pistol was out of the question. I couldn't even grip a pencil with these gnarled fingers. The best I could come up with was two bottles. One of diazepam (I had plenty for treating my leg spasms). The other was Black 33 overproof rum, which has a base alcohol content of nearly 80 percent. They waited out of sight on the floor of my van, in my backpack. Dusk settled on the red rocks, the sun fading behind a large butte. I was so very tired. Done. *I don't want to suffer anymore. There is no escape, no relief from this nightmare. This is my only option. I've betrayed the woman I love. They're all better off without me. God, let me just lie down. Let me die. Get it over with. I'm so tired.*

I must have dozed off, and when I opened my eyes, I thought I still wore my sunglasses. The lights of Sedona swam in front of me, making me nauseous. My head throbbed. *Damn it!* I was alive. Hopelessly alive. *The pain will never end. I've run out of ideas, I give up. There is no other way out of my problems. Imprisoned in this broken body that's unfixable.*

Night's chill had seeped in. I shivered and cursed. I'd forgotten to bring my Compazine. That would have helped keep me from vomiting once I started drinking my cocktail. I unlocked my chair and rolled back to grab my jacket. No sense in being uncomfortable, right? I thought to start the van too, and turn on the heater for a while. I picked up the backpack and rolled back into place at the steering wheel. Pulling the pills and rum out, I arranged them on the engine cover beside me. *Christ, it gets cold in the desert at night.* I turned the key. Nothing. No sound, not even a whir from the battery trying to kick in. *Double damn! Why now?* I looked at my watch; it was well past midnight. If the cocktail didn't do the job, the hypothermia would finish me off. I tried the ignition again. Still nothing. I couldn't even get out of the van without the electricity to run the lift. *This is it. This is the end. This isn't the way it's supposed to be — I can't even do* this *right! What's wrong with me? What a loser.*

A knock on my window startled me, interrupted my morose musings. A cop, peering in with his flashlight, told me to roll my window down.

I croaked as loud as I could: "Electric is out. The window won't roll down."

He went to the other side of the van and opened the passenger door, leaned over the seat, and scanned the dark cavity inside with his flashlight; he hesitated for a moment on the pills and bottle of rum on the engine cover between us.

"Are you all right, son?"

"Yeah. No, not really. My van won't start."

"I can help you with that. Got a buddy that runs an all-night towing business. He's a pretty good mechanic. Let me see if I can get him up here to take a look." He climbed into the passenger seat, like we were old friends on a road trip together, turned the two-way radio clipped to his shoulder to his face, and pressed the call button.

"Officer Juarez to Central. Over." A static-filled voice responded. "Assistance needed at Airport Mesa. Call Bubba's Tow Service. Over." More static and a faint "Copy that, Officer. Over."

"You'd think reception would be better than that on top of this butte, huh?" He grinned at me, a conspiratory gleam in his eyes. "Town's quiet tonight. I think I'll just sit here, take it easy until Joe shows up."

"Uh, sure. Okay." I choked on the words, wishing I could figure a way to get him out of the van. I felt guilty, like I was busted, but I hadn't even cracked open the rum.

He leaned forward, peeled his jacket off, detached the radio, and laid it on the dash in front of him. "You must be freezing." He leaned over and draped the jacket over my shoulders, tucking it around my arms like a bright yellow cocoon.

"Thanks." After a few minutes, I stopped shivering, was able to breathe easier.

"So. Here you are in the desert in the middle of the night. Got your cocktail ready. I take it things are pretty fucked up, huh?" He stared straight ahead, slouching and settling into the seat.

"Yeah." Still wary of his intentions, I wasn't ready to elaborate on my own intentions.

Juarez starting talking then, acknowledging that there are times in life when we might feel totally hopeless, helpless, and overwhelmed with emotional pain. It can seem like there is no other way out of our problems, we've run out of ideas, possible solutions. Our problems seem unfixable. The pain feels like it will never end. We believe we've run out of options, and doing ourselves in is the only answer left.

"I get it, son. I've been there before myself. My drinking drove my girlfriend away; I got worse. Even my foxhole prayers weren't working for me anymore. I wanted to get back at her, show her how much pain I was in. A buddy on the force helped me to see that suicide was a permanent solution to a temporary problem. You will get through the tunnel and come out on the other side."

That's when the dam broke. I told him about the accident, life as a quad for the past twenty-five years, the dating disasters, the psychotic home care employees, and Josephine. Told him that all my training as a counselor didn't amount to shit when it came to being able to cope with all of it. Told him I was just plain tired of fighting, of trying to find the strength to get through one more day.

"You've got through so far. You can get through the next hour. It's almost daylight now. We can go get some donuts and coffee when we get your van running."

I smiled feebly at his joke. I could see what he was doing, distracting me and getting me to focus on something else besides the pills and the rum. He seemed to read my mind, pointing to them.

"I don't really think you should do it. If you still want

someone to point you to the meaning of life, there are plenty of New Age nuts around here that will feed you manufacturer-approved thoughts so you can make a super-balanced decision about what to do with the rest of your life." Our eyes locked. I snickered and shook my head.

"Besides, you'll miss out on that next pizza. Have you thought of pizza?" That brought a belly laugh to the surface.

In the weak light of dawn, I spotted a hummingbird landing on desert scrub in front of the van. The hummer didn't care if I was dead or alive. His purpose in life was to collect pollen, and he was busy doing it. This tiny creature was just another "little thing" yet so incredibly beautiful. I was alive and there at that moment to see it.

"Anna's Hummingbird. They usually show up here in the fall and winter," Juarez whispered.

I realized then, I had a destiny and only I could fulfill it or waste it. On this planet, I, too, am just a tiny creature with the same massive potential. I felt a tear slip away and grinned at Juarez. I'd taken the dark-tinted glasses off. I'd go with him to eat donuts and drink coffee. And I'd drive home again in the morning's sunlight.

Acknowledgements

First, many thanks to my fellow students from the long-ago Night Owls writing class – Nancy Brook, Martin Peterson and Cheryl Mosely - where we met and formed the original Night Writers. I'm forever beholden to you, my friends, for humoring me with my first attempts at writing.

My gratitude also goes out to my teacher, Russell Rowland. Dear friend, you so kindly offered your time and guidance to me as I struggled to master the assignments in your writing classes. Those many evenings that we spent around your dining room table are priceless. I would not have had the courage to pursue the writer's craft without the inspiration that you and your other students so generously gave to me.

In regard to my family, I'm forever grateful for my mom, Vivian, our historian who indulged me while I incessantly badgered her with my tape recorder. It's such a gift, to still hear her voice when I play it back from time to time. Likewise, I'm indebted to my brother Deith for supplying me with lots of material from the growing-up years, and for being my "ghost writer" on several chapters – thanks for contributing your masterful prose! And, of course, my deep admiration for my brother Ward, who loved to write and was a budding author in his own right. I'm blessed to have found his stories amongst his belongings and that my family so graciously allowed me to be the keeper of those priceless papers.

In addition, I'm thankful for my husband Charlie, my lovely daughters Erika and Brooke, my Mom-in-Law Dorothy, and many steadfast friends for always believing in me. For nearly a decade, they've asked me, "How's the book coming along?" And for nearly a decade I've replied, "I just need to add a chapter here or there, and then it will be done!"

Finally, Kings and Cowboys is a reality in large part due to the perseverance of the staff at Outskirts Press. Despite my repeated insistence that the manuscript was not yet finished, they gently nudged me along for months on end, aware that authors never know when to stop.

At long last, I have put the pen down and stepped away, trusting that whatever happens now is in the hands of providence. This story has come full circle, and I'm taking bets on the next tall tale.